To Donn

Enjoy
2012

# LEAP YEAR

To Donna

# Leap Year
## Be Scared...
## Be *Very* Scared...

By Daniel M. Warloch

Strategic Book Group
Durham, Connecticut

© 2010 by Daniel M. Warloch
All rights reserved. First edition 2010.

No part of this book may be reproduced or transmitted in any form or by any means, graphic, electronic, or mechanical, including photocopying, recording, taping, or by any information storage retrieval system, without the permission, in writing, from the publisher. This book is a work of fiction. Names and characters are of the author's imagination or are used fictitiously. Any resemblance to an actual person, living or dead, is entirely coincidental.

Strategic Book Group
P. O. Box 333
Durham, CT 06422
http://www.strategicbookclub.com

ISBN: 978-1-60976-075-5

Book Design by Julius Kiskis

Printed in the United States of America
18 17 16 15 14 13 12 11 10     1 2 3 4 5

# Acknowledgments

Special thanks go to Barbara Maltas and all the pupils of Class TGV 2009/2010 at Hoole Church of England Primary School, Chester for their kind comments and constructive criticisms during the course of writing this novel.

Not forgetting my wife, June, and my two sons Lee and Mark for all their help and advice. And, last but not least, the stars of the novel: my grandchildren, James, Thomas, and Jordan.

# Preface

Jordan, James, and Thomas Waldron lived with their parents in the small village of Prenton, fifteen miles outside of Chester. Jordan was the eldest at twelve; James, known as Squirrel by his close friends because he tended to store odd objects in his coat pockets, was ten; and Thomas had just turned eight. Jordan tolerated his younger brothers most of the time; yet he would always keep a watchful eye over them while at school or when out playing with the small number of children who hung around their neighborhood.

One of James's Christmas presents had been a state of the art four-man tent from his Nana, but unfortunately, because of the continually cold weather, he hadn't had the chance to use it. Eventually, after James's constant badgering, his parents reluctantly agreed to allow them to sleep out in the back garden, providing Jordan promised to watch over his two younger brothers, which Jordan begrudgingly agreed to do.

# Chapter One

*February 28, 2008, 9:00 p.m.*
*The Waldron's Back Garden*

"I'm warning you, Jordan. If you don't let me come with you, I'll tell Mum and Dad," whispered James, staring at his older brother, who was hopping around on one foot in the small confines of their tent, struggling to slip on his jeans.

"This is my dare, not yours, and keep your voice down, will you? You'll wake Thomas up," ordered Jordan, glancing down at Thomas, who was beginning to stir.

"What's all the whispering about?" asked a bleary-eyed Thomas, his head suddenly popping out from the top of his sleeping bag.

"Great, look what you've gone and done now, James. You've woken Tom up. Go back to sleep, both of you, before Mum and Dad come out to check what the fuss is all about," snapped Jordan, stretched out on the floor of the tent with his back arched up, fighting with the zip of his jeans.

"What dare are you talking about, Jordan? It's not Billy Three Hats picking on you again, is it?" queried Thomas, suddenly becoming interested in the discussion.

"Yes, it is Billy, and he isn't picking on me. Also, I'd make sure he doesn't hear you calling him Billy Three Hats, or he will probably punch you on the nose for saying it," hissed Jordan, safely tucking his cell phone inside the pocket of his jeans.

"Jordan, why do you call him Billy Th . . . Th . . . thing-a-ma-jig anyway?" stuttered James, shuffling around inside his sleeping bag, attempting to make himself more comfortable.

"Because sometimes, if you haven't already noticed, he likes to wear a silly red bandana under his baseball cap, and then pulls the hood of his coat over his head," muttered Jordan, who was now becoming annoyed with his little brother.

"A banana on his head?" roared James and Thomas, rolling around in fits of laughter on the floor of the tent.

"I said a bandana, you stupid idiots, not a banana. It's like a large handkerchief that you have to tie in a knot to keep from falling off your head. And be quiet, both of you, as I don't want Mum and Dad to find out what I'm up to," snickered Jordan, imagining a banana balanced on top of Billy's head.

Once the giggling had died down, Jordan zipped his jacket up to his chin, pulled his collar up, and when he was satisfied that he had everything he needed for the long, cold night, began to carefully crawl on his hands and knees toward the front of the tent. Sweaters and thick blankets had been wedged down in between their sleeping bags, and there were at least a dozen fluff-coated hard-boiled sweets and empty crisp packets scattered around the floor. In addition to all of this clutter, there was also an assortment of children's paperback horror novels strewn about on the floor of the tent that they'd been reading earlier on in the evening.

"If James is going with you, I am too . . . Jordan, where are you going?" inquired Thomas, suddenly becoming excited with the prospect of an adventure in the dark with his two older brothers.

"Look, listen up, you two, and get this through your thick skulls, you are not coming with me, so button it and leave me alone," growled Jordan, gingerly unzipping the flaps of the tent, listening out for anyone who may have been coming out of the back door to investigate the racket they'd been making.

"MUM!" shouted James.

"What's up with you now?" called out their mother through the open kitchen window.

"Mum, Jordan's . . ." James abruptly stopped mid-sentence, because Jordan had quickly covered his mouth, preventing him from giving the game away.

"If you don't behave yourselves, I won't be taking you Ten Pin Bowling tomorrow," shouted their mother.

"And what's Jordan up to?"

"I was only being silly Mum, frightening James and Thomas with a ghost story. I've stopped now," lied Jordan, removing his hand from James's slavering wet lips, wiping away the dribble from the palm of his hand down the front of his jacket. James wiped his mouth with the back of his hand and blew a raspberry at Jordan.

A faint smile slipped across Jordan's face.

"Goodnight, and I don't want to hear another word from either of you for the rest of the night; if I do, you can all come back in the house. Do you understand?" their Mum threatened, as she carried on washing the dishes from supper.

"Yes, Mum, and goodnight," echoed the three boys.

A cheeky smile passed between them as they listened to the mournful gusting wind playing with the sides of the tent.

"Well, are we going or not?" whispered James, scrambling out of his sleeping bag, grabbing ahold of his crumpled-up jeans, which he'd been using as a pillow, examining the dozens of creases. "Never mind; no one's going to see them." Chuckling to himself under his breath, he puffed a cloud of moisture before him.

"Come on then, Jordan, where are we going?" asked Thomas, his voice muffled as he was struggling to pull two sweaters over his head at the same time.

"The dare is for me to sleep in the old lodge by the

main gate to Thorngarth Hall, from ten tonight until sunrise tomorrow," confessed Jordan, studying their terrified looking faces. "So . . . do you both still want to come along with me, or are you now having cold feet, as Dad would say?"

"Cool," answered Thomas, the look of fear plastered all over his innocent looking face. Thomas was a suspicious little boy, so he thought it might be a good idea to rub the nose of his favorite teddy bear for luck, as he was scared.

"Oh boy . . . now that is one mean dare, Jordan," stated James, wondering whether it may have been best if he stayed within the safety and warmth of the tent.

"Come on, James, I can't imagine anything awful happening to us if we stick together," remarked Thomas, trying to sound brave. "And if we put on enough socks, we won't have cold feet . . . will we?" His witticism brought out further fits of laughter, resulting in them quickly burying their heads in the blankets and sleeping bags for fear of their parents hearing them.

## Chapter Two

Thorngarth Hall had been built in the late 1800s by the Duke of Cheshire as a weekend retreat where he entertained the rich and famous within its exquisitely decorated rooms, along with its extensive landscaped gardens and manicured lawns. The single-story lodge was added on as an afterthought by the Duke for his servants to reside in, and was positioned 100 meters from the hall, adjacent to the main gate.

The Duke died in 1920, leaving the estate to his only son. In the following years, the son never bothered with the upkeep of the hall, preferring to live the high life in London, ultimately leaving the hall and its grounds to end up in a rundown state.

During the early 1960s, a middle-aged twin brother and sister purchased Thorngarth Hall and lodge. After twelve exhausting months, they had managed to renovate the lodge for the twins to live in while converting the bottom two floors of the hall into an orphanage for underprivileged children in the local area. Yet, on one freezing winters morning, February 29, 1968 (a leap year), the brother and sister, along with its twenty deprived children, mysteriously vanished. After a six-month-long fruitless investigation, the authorities decided to abandon the search, and to this day, no one had a clue of what became of them.

Since then, the hall had fallen into disrepair. The windows were boarded up with heavy-duty timber. The twisted rusting gates were kept tightly closed by a heavy chain coiled around the metal bars, securely fastened by a chunky metal padlock in the vain hope of preventing anyone from entering the grounds. The winding stone steps, which lead up to the main entrance to the hall, had been overrun with moss and weeds, giving the impression of a thick green stair carpet. Over the years, the gardens had become heavily overgrown; the branches of the six-foot high hedges looked to be tied together in knots, and the thorns and brambles seemed to be snaking around the thick exposed roots. Razor-wire had been crudely erected around what was left of the old wooden guttering around the hall. The only inhabitants now were nesting birds in the eaves. Some of the local residents even claimed that they had seen bats entering and leaving from the uppermost part of the hall, and sometimes—when they were really desperate—tramps roamed the grounds, and occasionally entered the hall. But for some unknown reason, never ended up sleeping there the whole night.

On February 28, 1980 (a leap year), a young brother and sister mysteriously disappeared in the area bordering the hall, resulting in a widespread manhunt of the outlying district, involving hundreds of volunteers from the public, along with the police and search-and-rescue teams based nearby in the Welsh mountains.

This was the reason why Jordan had been given the dare for him to spend the night at the lodge.

To this day, *those* children have never been found . . .

## Chapter Three

Once they were all wrapped up in the new waterproof padded jackets each of them had been given for Christmas, they carefully arranged pillows and blankets inside their sleeping bags, giving the illusion that there was someone tucked up fast asleep inside.

It was bitterly cold outside; the night sky was thick with churning snow clouds, and the blustery wind was causing the dead leaves and discarded sweet wrappers to end up in the dirt-encrusted snow that had been piled up in their small back garden. Slivers of light spilled out through the kitchen window, bathing the tent in a ghostly glow, and the snow shone and glittered in the moonlight.

Without uttering a word, Jordan pushed the flaps to one side, letting in a gust of freezing air, followed by a flurry of snowflakes. After sneakily exiting the tent, their breath clouding in the damp evening air, Jordan securely zipped it up. Thomas, meanwhile, was up on his tiptoes, craning his neck, attempting to see through the kitchen window and ensuring that their Mum didn't come out to check on them. Satisfied that the coast was clear, the three boys stood frozen to the spot, scanning each other's faces, all wondering whether it would be best for them to go back to the tent and the coziness of their sleeping bags.

"Well, what are you waiting for, Jordan?" asked James, cupping his gloved hands and blowing into them. "Do you intend standing out here in the back garden all night like frozen snowmen? You're not chickening out now, are you?"

"No. I'm not chickening out. So come on then, and no moaning on the way, okay?" replied Jordan, stamping his feet on the packed snow, trying to warm his cold toes.

As their breath frosted and hung in the air, somewhere in the distance an owl hooted and a dog barked in the night. The snow slowly cascaded toward them; giant feathery flakes tumbled down from the heavy sky, settling with a whisper on their hair and clothes. James and Thomas stood and stared at one another beneath a swirling flurry of snow, hands dug firmly inside their coat pockets.

It was James who eventually broke the cold, stony silence. "As Thomas said before . . . what can possibly happen to us?" he declared, wheeling around to face the wooden gate that would ultimately lead them out of the garden.

Under the cover of darkness, and the stillness of the night, the three boys were just beginning an adventure they thought could only happen to other children in horror books.

## Chapter Four

"Brrrr, it's freezing. Are we nearly there yet, Jordan?" asked a shivering James, trying to rub some warmth into his chilled arms, his breath pluming before him in the crisp night air.

"We should be there soon, but if you don't stop complaining, you can both go back to the tent," replied Jordan, puffing air into his cold hands to keep them warm.

They were finding it difficult at first, trudging through the ridges and ankle-deep mountains of snow that had been thrown up by the side of the road by the snow ploughs during the course of the day.

"How will Billy what's-his-name know you've stayed in the lodge all night, Jordan?" queried James, rubbing his gloved hands together, trying to circulate the blood around his chilled fingers.

Jordan glanced across at James and smiled before answering. "That's what I was wondering earlier this evening. But now that you two are here, you can both vouch for me, can't you?" answered Jordan, clapping his hands together to circulate the blood around his cold fingers.

"I suppose we could—if you made it worth our while," replied James, sneaking a cheeky look at Jordan from out of the corner of his eye.

"Don't push your luck, James," chuckled Jordan, his lips almost blue from the biting wind.

"If Dad was with us now, what would he say?" interrupted Thomas, flapping his arms about like a bird, trying to keep himself warm.

"'Keep your wits about you!'" all three shouted, chasing each other around in circles, trying to push one another into the piles of slushy snow. After five exhausting, giddy minutes, they eventually called a truce, brushing off as much of the snow from their clothes and hair, and then carrying on slipping and sliding their way up the road toward the lodge.

Jordan took the lead, walking a few paces in front, stopping now and again, and listening out for any unusual noises. Beneath their small footsteps, the ground was becoming thicker and thicker by the minute from the constant snowfall. The streets were eerily quiet and still; street lamps were buzzing softly amid the hiss and patter of the persistent heavy snowfall.

"Keep your eyes open. I wouldn't be surprised if Billy came charging out from over there," warned Jordan, indicating with a nod of his head to a cluster of bushes over to his right.

"How do you expect us to walk without falling over if

we don't have our eyes open? You nutcase," laughed James, tossing a slushy snowball over in Jordan's direction.

"You know what I meant, squirrel head," snickered Jordan, squatting down and scooping up a pile of snow, throwing it at James.

While toiling through the thick snow, the weather had suddenly turned cold and blustery, causing the wind to whine and wail like a banshee through the trees, and the bare branches were beginning to dance and shake. Their surroundings resembled a magical winter wonderland scene created by the orange neon glow spilling down from the street lamps.

They constantly peered through the sinister shadows of the trees, expecting to see Billy jump out at them, screaming and waving his arms around like a mad man.

"Thomas, will you hurry up? I knew it would be a bad idea bringing you two along," called out Jordan, waiting impatiently for Thomas to reach him.

"Shut u-u-p, Jordan, and d-d-don't be s-s-so bossy. Thomas's legs are s-s-smaller than ours; give him time t-t-t-o catch us up," said James, the cold making him stammer, and licking his lips as they had become dry and chapped.

Suddenly, a cat sprang out from the shadows of the bushes, causing their hearts to jump into their mouths. They instinctively opened their mouths to scream, but nothing came out, only their breath drifting in the cold, damp air. They stared at each other, trying to control their breathing. Thomas staggered back and slumped to his knees in the compacted snow, burying his face in his gloved hands, shaking his head. After a few heart-stopping seconds, Jordan and James leapt across the mounds of snow toward Thomas to check on him.

Thomas tilted his head and smiled up at them.

"Are you okay, Tom?" asked a concerned Jordan, placing a hand on his shoulder and squeezing gently.

"Stupid blooming cat . . . I nearly had a squeaky behind," giggled Thomas, easing himself off the wet floor, his breath coming out in white clouds.

Jordan and James began to laugh as they bent down to help Thomas up to his feet.

They decided to rest a while on an ice-covered wall to settle their nerves, the cold air chilling their lungs when they took a deep breath.

Having controlled their breathing and composure, they set off once again through the deep snow. The wind had suddenly sprung up again, forcing the trees to bend so that they looked as if they were performing a macabre dance, with their branches resembling gnarled wagging fingers.

At last, after ten exhausting, jittery minutes, they reached the twisted rusting gate by the entrance to the grounds of the hall. Luckily for them, there was sufficient light from the moon to see their way up the path leading to the front door of the lodge.

"It seems as though someone's been here recently by

the look of the footprints in the snow and the dozens of tracks leading into the lodge," stated Thomas, squatting down to examine the well-trodden snow.

"That's odd," remarked Jordan, looking slightly puzzled.

"What's the matter, Jordan?" inquired Thomas, his face as white as the snow on the ground.

"The footprints and tracks are mine—well, some of them are at least. But I don't remember making that many . . . oh, never mind! I must be mistaken, that's all. Anyway, to put both your minds at ease, I came down here this afternoon. I wasn't planning on sleeping in this dump all night without blankets and something to eat. I also brought some newspapers along with me from home. I also managed to collect some twigs on the way, which we can use to start a small fire, just in case it gets cold during the night." Jordan informed them, deep in thought.

"Good thinking, Batman," laughed James, looking up at his older brother in awe, shifting from one foot to another.

Jordan was concerned about the additional footprints and tracks they'd found, yet he didn't want to say anything about them to James and Thomas, as they may have become frightened, and decided to go back home.

Satisfied that there were no unwelcome guests hiding in any of the bushes or silently creeping up from behind, they stamped the snow off their soaked sneakers and shuffled through the yawning mouth of the entrance to the lodge. Stepping into the dark enclosure of the hallway, it took them a moment for their eyes to become accustomed to the darkness. It would have been pitch black inside if it wasn't for a faint light, intermittently cast by the moon as the heavy snow clouds scudded across the sky.

Once they had entered the gloomy interior, they saw before them a large chamber, showing various signs of decay and neglect. One wall was dominated by empty floor-to-ceiling bookshelves, which looked to be completely infested with either wood rot or wood worm, and the wall opposite was graffiti-sprayed with what resembled children's crude drawings. A discarded well-worn sofa had been laid on its side in one corner, with most of its stuffing spilling out onto the dusty wooden floor.

"I won't be sleeping on that tonight," remarked James, moving away to the next room, hoping to find something more comfortable and welcoming to sleep on.

Within seconds of them entering the adjoining room, James and Thomas were pulled back by a sudden jolt from Jordan.

"Sssh! Just hold it there, both of you. I thought I heard something moving around over there," whispered Jordan, gesturing to the spot with a jerk of his head.

The three of them suddenly had the horrible sensation of a spider crawling up their spines, the hairs on the back of their necks standing up as though they wanted to pop out of their skin. Sweat trickled down their backs, causing them to shiver with fright.

Quickly adjusting their eyes to the inky darkness, yet not being able to make out a great deal of what was in front of them through the gloom, the brothers reached out and fumbled in the dark, finding each other's probing hands and grasping them tightly. They then stared at the glowing yellow orbs, peering at them from within the darkness of the room.

"Jordan, what is it? I'm frightened," whimpered Thomas, realizing he was crying, and trying very hard to send the message from his brain to his legs for them to move, with very little success.

The color had drained out of James's face, and he'd clenched his teeth to stop himself from crying out. All he could hear was his own breathing and the sound of his heart thumping in his chest.

Jordan had tensed up, expecting the worse, remembering the additional footprints and disturbed snow by the entrance. He bit his bottom lip; tears of panic were slowly starting to roll down his cheeks.

Blinking as their eyes adjusted to the darkness, they saw something move. The faintest flash of something pale, flitting from one dark place to another.

## Chapter Five

A hush descended over the room, and for a split second, not one of them dared move or utter a word. Then, without any kind of warning, a large mud-spattered dog brushed passed them with a speed that took them by surprise. They hastily moved to one side to avoid being knocked over in its haste to escape. Unfortunately, due to the combination of the dog scampering out to freedom and the brothers frantically trying to dodge away, they stirred up all the dust, which had been coating the floor for the past years, causing it to float around the dark confines of the room. All three sneezed several times as the dust irritated them and their eyes began to water. They wiped away the tears with the back of their hands, leaving black streaks crisscrossing their faces, creating the effect of three commandos on a night's reconnaissance mission.

"I want to go home Jordan, I don't like it here," said Thomas with a cough, choking on the dust that was coating the back of his throat, twin tracks of tears rolling down his dirt-smeared cheeks.

"There's nothing to worry about; it was only a silly

dog hiding inside the lodge to keep warm. Please just listen to me, Tom: Once we've made our beds up for the night, and shared out the biscuits I've stored along with the blankets, you'll feel much better, you'll see," pleaded Jordan, hoping he didn't have to go all the way back home with him. "I'll start the fire to keep us all warm in an old fireplace I spotted when I came down here this afternoon, so what do you say to that?" he added, hoping it would help the situation they'd found themselves in.

"Hey, look, guys, I've brought my flashlight along with me, so we can have some additional light to see what we're doing," announced James, snapping it on, the beam forming weird shadows along the dust-covered floor and graffiti-covered wall.

"Why didn't you use it when we first arrived, you idiot?" fumed Jordan. The look on his face could have turned anyone to stone.

"Because you didn't ask me if I had one, poo- head," snapped James, causing a ripple of laughter, easing some of the tension in the room.

"James, keep the beam pointed over toward the fireplace while I get the fire going, and once we're all wrapped up like bugs-in-a-rug, I'll hand out the biscuits. Then we can settle down for the rest of the night, and James, you'd be best turning the flashlight off when we've finished, as we don't want to use up the batteries," suggested Jordan, trying to make his two younger brothers feel both relaxed and safe.

Ten minutes later, Jordan had cleared most of the damp ash and shards of soot-coated bricks from the bottom of the iron grate. He snapped the twigs with several loud and brittle cracks, carefully placing them around the bottom of the grate along with a handful of scrunched up newspapers.

Meanwhile, James and Thomas were busy sweeping to one side the accumulation of ceiling plaster and strips of curled up crispy wallpaper from the floor with their soaking wet sneakers, hoping to give them an area that was clear of rubble for their makeshift beds.

"Jordan, what happens if someone comes walking by and notices the smoke coming out of the chimney? They might think the lodge is on fire and decide to call the fire department. Then what do we do?" asked a worried James.

"I wouldn't worry too much about that, James; it's only a small fire, so the smoke will only trickle out of the chimney. I don't think anyone would notice. Like I've said before, don't worry; everything will be fine, you wait and see," replied Jordan, carefully striking one of the matches, putting the flame to the collection of paper and broken twigs. James opened his mouth to argue, and then shut it again and gave a tiny shrug before continuing to clear away the dirt from the dusty floor. By this time, Thomas was eager to share the biscuits then go to sleep, as he had suddenly become hungry and sleepy.

With the fire nicely blazing, the flames constantly crackling and hissing from the twigs and newspapers—Jordan had made sure they were positioned well away from the sparks that were floating about—he began to share the assortment of biscuits.

Suddenly, the slightest noise coming from outside made them jump out of their skins. But after a few nervous minutes of constantly scanning the room and the area immediately outside in the hallway for any other nasty surprises, they began to settle down into their respective crude beds, preparing themselves for a long, cold, and spooky night.

Small tongues of orange flames chased dancing flakes of ash up the chimney, and the flickering glow of the fire played on their dirty faces.

## Chapter Six

"Jordan, do you think Mum will notice we're missing?" asked James, carefully checking through his pockets for anything that would come in handy for fighting off any monsters that might suddenly appear in the night.

"I hope not, and I can't imagine her sticking her head inside the tent. She could just call out to see if we are all fast asleep, and when there's no reply, hopefully she will go back inside," Jordan assumed, trying to sound convincing.

"Jordan, I want to go to the toilet. Will you come with me?" asked a nervous and frightened Thomas.

"Oh, Tom, we've only been settled a few minutes, can't it wait?" grumbled Jordan, tapping the embers of the fire with a stick, causing hundreds of tiny red sparks to rise and float up the chimney.

It was then that the floodgates opened, with Thomas sobbing his eyes out, his head buried deep inside his blanket, crying for his Mum.

"Okay, okay, Thomas, I'll take you, and I'm sorry for shouting . . . but hurry up about it, as I don't want to be hanging around too long if I can help it. It's freezing out there," groaned Jordan, now feeling guilty about his outburst.

"I want to go as well, Jordan," chimed in James, tossing his blanket to one side and springing to his feet.

"Oh crap! I knew it would be a bad idea to bring you two along," groaned Jordan through gritted teeth.

"What was that you said, Jordan?" questioned James, knowing full well what his older brother had said.

"Nothing; just talking to myself," replied Jordan, gesturing with a sweep of his hand for James to move to the front of the line, reminding him that he was in charge of the flashlight.

With a hint of concern across his face, James strode past Jordan and Thomas toward the opening of the door, the beam dancing through the inky darkness into the hallway in front of him.

Satisfied that there was no one around, they stared out into the snowy landscape of the grounds. The carpet of snow on the ground and the pillows of snow on every laden branch seemed to radiate by the quicksilver glow of the moon around them.

They began to trudge through the thick snow toward a secluded tree over to their left— in clear sight of the hall. The bare branches above them were coated with undisturbed snow, like icing on a children's birthday cake, and in the distance the characteristic sounds of church bells were beginning to strike midnight. A light breeze was teasing the firs and spruces, and the swaying of the branches was producing a chorus of whispers and creaks in the background, which made the boys stop and stare amongst the surrounding trees and hedges. Not wanting to be seen by anyone who may have been walking past out on the main road, they moved further along toward a thick copse of trees, their branches drooping, all heavily laden with snow.

"Hey guys, just look over there; the moonlight's reflecting in the windows of the hall, can you see?" James announced then quickly stopped in his tracks, realizing what he'd just said. "Just hold on a minute, you two, how can there be a reflection from the moon coming off wood? If I remember correctly, there shouldn't to be any glass in the windows of the hall," he continued, shuffling his feet in the snow. A chill shot down his spine, and even though it was bitterly cold, sweat was beginning to form on his forehead.

"Come on, let's go over and check it out," suggested Jordan, trying to put on a brave face. "It must be just a trick of the light, that's all . . . well, are you coming or not? Or are you a couple of scaredy cats?"

Without a second thought, Jordan pushed the bushes and brambles to one side, dislodging a small cascade of powdery snow onto his hair and shoulders, and steadily made his way toward the smooth undisturbed snow-covered path leading to the hall.

"Jordan, please don't go; I'm scared," pleaded

Thomas, sliding his back down one of the trees to the cold damp ground, pulling his legs up to his chest and resting his forehead on his knees.

Aware that Thomas was frightened, Jordan and James quickly made their way across to sit down next to him, hoping to give him some words of comfort.

"I'm not frightened," said James, trying to sound brave, wrapping his arm around Thomas's shoulder.

"Come on, Thomas," begged Jordan, smiling. "We'll just nip over for a few minutes, that's all, and then we'll come straight back here to the lodge. No, I tell you what, we'll head off back to the tent, what do you say to that?"

Wiping his nose with the back of his hand—giving a fair impression of someone pulling out a foot from a muddy bog—Thomas glanced up at them both, smiled, lifted himself up off the wet floor, and bravely made his way toward the hall, calling over his shoulder on the way, giggling to himself. "Come on then, what are you waiting for? You couple of sissies."

After that surprising turn of events, Jordan and James quickly eased themselves up from the soggy floor and trotted across toward Thomas. They began to playfully ruffle Thomas's hair for being so cheeky, and once again they exploded in a fresh peal of laughter.

With an exerted sweaty effort, they cautiously and steadily made their way through the thick snow up the long-winding stone path, which would eventually lead them to the large, dark, and awesome "newly restored" building, unaware of what was in store for them.

## Chapter Seven

By the time they had reached the snow-covered path bordering the unwelcoming, sinister hall, they were shivering from the cold, their teeth were beginning to chatter, and the biting wind was trying its best to tear the jackets from their backs.

"Jord-d-dan, I can s-s-see a s-s-small amount of l-l-light coming from one of the w-w-windows over th-th-there," stammered James, chewing his bottom lip and pointing his cold, shaky finger toward the side of the building.

"S-s-h-h," whispered Jordan, shivering from the cold. "I think I c-c-can hear voices c-c-coming from th-th-the inside."

"There's . . . glass . . . in . . . the . . . windows . . . Jordan," whimpered James, his face ashen with shock. "Also, g-g-guys . . . look what's h-h-happened to the rest of the building; it isn't in ruins anymore . . . Jordan, I'm n-n-not too happy about all of this; what h-h-have you got us in-to-to?"

"I'm as p-p-puzzled as you are, b-b-but I'm sure there's a logical explanation," stuttered Jordan, aware that it hadn't been such a good idea in the first place to snoop around. He hadn't wanted to say anything for fear of frightening his two younger brothers.

Accepting Jordan's unconvincing answer, James and Thomas glided across to stand close to one another for comfort and trap whatever body heat there was between them, as they were both frozen stiff.

"It must be a d-d-dream, and we'll s-s-soon wake up in the m-m-morning in our sleeping b-b-bags," declared James, nipping himself on the back of his hand, checking to see if he was asleep or not. Feeling the sudden pain, James chose to ignore it, deciding to keep his thoughts to himself.

Thomas wasn't too bothered about what was happening around him, as he had his two older brothers with him for protection.

Some minutes later, they were standing beneath one of the soot-streaked leaded windows, the faint eerie glow filtering through, giving them enough light to see what they were doing. With a great deal of effort, they stood on their tiptoes, stretching their necks, attempting to see what was going on inside; unfortunately, none of them could. Then out of the blue, coming from the inside of the building, they heard the sounds of children singing.

"Ugh! It reminds me of a school assembly," whispered James, his eyes taking on a haunting look.

Jordan and Thomas raised their eyes and nodded their agreement.

"Thomas, come over here so I can lift you up, and

then you may be able to see what's happening inside," suggested Jordan, lacing his gloved fingers together to form a foot hold, then bending down slightly, trying to make it easy for Thomas to slip his foot in.

"No way, Jordan. James can do it; he's taller than me," replied a troubled Thomas, backing away slightly from the wall, hands buried deep in his coat pockets.

"Wicked," whispered James, moving closer to Jordan. "Thomas, if you're too scared to climb up, at least come over and give me a hand so I won't fall over," ordered James, suddenly feeling courageous.

James carefully placed his right foot in Jordan's cupped hands and steadied himself by gripping hold of the wall with his left hand. With Thomas's assistance, he managed to reach up and grab ahold of the crumbling brickwork before pulling himself up with both hands, hoping he would be high enough to peer inside the room unobserved.

As soon as he was at eye level with the bottom of the windowsill, he quickly ducked down, not wanting to be spotted by anyone inside the room.

"What can you see, James?" asked a cold and impatient Thomas.

"The room seems to be full of scruffy looking kids singing. Also, I'm not entirely certain, but I thought I spotted two giants walking out of the room . . . it looks really creepy in there, guys," mumbled James, leaning over slightly so his brothers could hear what he was saying without him having to shout.

Making certain he wasn't going to fall in a heap in the thick snow, James began to slowly ease himself down to the ground, grabbing hold of Thomas and Jordan's shoulders for support.

They exchanged a few nervous glances before Jordan piped up with an idea.

"Come on, you two; let's try and find a way of getting inside the hall," he proposed, forcing a smile.

"Jordan!" exclaimed James, carefully wiping away the buildup of snow from his eyelashes. "Have you suddenly gone stark raving mad? This place has been abandoned for years; then all of a sudden, there is a load of weirdo kids inside, plus two humungous individuals, who I definitely don't want to bump into, and glass in the window frames. And for some unexplained reason, which, at this moment in time I can't figure out, the whole building and its surroundings have surprisingly come back to life, and you want us to go inside . . . no way, man!"

"You can go in and check it out if you want to, Jordan; we're heading off back to the tent," muttered James, wrapping his arm around Thomas's shoulder, slowly moving away from the side of the building.

"James, Thomas, I don't want to go in there all by myself; please come back. Hey, just think what our mates at school will say when we tell them what we've been up to," implored Jordan, with a hint of a smile across his cold, cheeky face.

They knew they couldn't let Jordan go in there all by himself. They were brothers, after all, always looking after one another.

There was a moment's awkward silence while they considered what Jordan had said.

It was Thomas who spoke up first.

"Come on, James. I can't imagine anything horrible happening to us if we stick together," he said, glancing back over his shoulder at Jordan, feeling both nervous and frightened about what could be waiting for them in the hall.

All of a sudden, it was as silent as a graveyard. The children inside the hall had suddenly stopped singing, which abruptly brought the three of them out of their mischievous thoughts.

Without uttering another word, they pushed their way through the thick blanket of snow toward the front of the hall, searching for a way in, feeling both excited and a little uneasy.

## Chapter Eight

The continuous heavy snowfall, combined with the strong gusting wind, had left a large bank of snow up against the sides of the porch at the entrance to the hall. There was so much snow piled up, they were finding it difficult at first to clear it away with their cold hands.

The first thing they uncovered was a rusted gargoyle door knocker, which was hanging from a single, heavy nail at its center. And somewhat eerily, it had a big smile on its ugly face stretching from one ear to the other.

"I've found the door handle, guys; are you ready?" Jordan informed them, leaning his shoulder against the door, hoping he didn't have to push too hard for it to open. "And we'd better get a move on; it's starting to snow heavily again. We can't afford to get our clothes any wetter than they're already are."

James and Thomas stared at each other, eyes like saucers, and went across to assist Jordan.

With very little effort, the door slowly eased open, the noise of the squeaking dry hinges echoing all around them. The draft pouring out through the small gap caused the dust motes to float around in the musty air, giving the effect of a light snowfall coming from the inside of the building.

"Jordan, did you happen to see the smiling face on the door knocker?" questioned James, looking troubled. "The ones I've seen before haven't been smiling; they normally have horrible, ugly faces. Do you think it's smiling because we're going to be trapped inside?" James's imagination was now running like crazy.

"Don't be so daft, James. Here, let me take a look," said Jordan, squeezing past to check it out for himself. "It looks to me as though it's a happy smiling face. Don't worry, door knockers can't hurt you!" replied Jordan. But he could have sworn that there was something odd about its expression—as though it was quietly amused by their unexpected appearance.

Before slipping between the gap of the door into the hall, Thomas stopped to sneakily glance up at the gruesome looking door knocker. He stood on his tiptoes to reach up and rub its crooked nose for luck. He also had his fingers crossed for added luck. "I think I'll cross my eyes, just in case, as you never know what could be lurking about inside," he whispered to no one in particular, as he was now scared . . . *very* scared!

Mindful that the squeaking of the dry rusty hinges on the door may have alerted anyone inside, the boys quickly eased it shut. Jordan decided to leave a wide enough gap for them to slide a hand around the edge so they could open it, just in case they needed to get out in an almighty hurry. They then dived for cover behind a large dusty pair of thick, heavy curtains hanging over to their left, ensuring that no one was likely to spot them if they happened to come out and investigate the noise they'd just made.

Certain no one was coming out from any of the downstairs rooms, they stealthily trooped down the long, dusty corridor, staying as close to the wood-paneled wall as possible and keeping a sharp look out for any unexpected company.

"Did anyone think to count the number of windows from the entrance when we were outside, so we'll know which room the children are in?" inquired James, looking across at his two brothers.

"I did," chirped up Thomas, raising his hand as though he was in class. "It was the sixth window . . . I counted them all."

Tiptoeing nervously on down the dimly lit corridor, wincing every time they stepped on a creaking floorboard, they were astounded by the size of the hallway, also spotting a wooden staircase positioned down the right-hand side that spiraled into the darkness above. Glancing up to the ceiling, they spied two large crystal chandeliers, each ablaze with candles, giving off a warm glow around the grand hallway. They stopped now and again to admire a number of black and white framed photographs hanging on both sides of the corridor—each depicting the hall just after it had been originally built. They sensed that the corridor seemed to go on forever and ever and ever . . .

Seconds later, they drew to a halt outside the room, which they calculated should belong to the sixth window across. Each of them placed an ear to the door, listening out for any movement coming from the inside. It was at this point that James decided he'd had enough, and he wanted to go back home.

"Come on, Jordan, I don't think this is a very good idea of yours, do *you*? We can't just walk in uninvited into someone else's house . . . the owners may think we are going to steal something." His voice edged with tension; his eyes were darting from one end of the corridor to the other. "And I feel that there is something horribly wrong about this place, especially if I was correct about those two ogres I spotted leaving the room," he added, slowly inching his way from the door.

"James, don't be such a big softy," scoffed Jordan, glancing over his shoulder. "Those two 'ogres' you noticed through that filthy window were most likely your own reflection. The light wasn't all that good for you to see clearly inside the room, now was it?"

"I'm not a softy, Jordan, and I *did* see something in . . ."

It was the sudden opening of the classroom door into the corridor that caused James to quickly stop talking. To their astonishment, a number of excited rag-tag looking children—who seemed to be wearing old shabby clothes, with clear evidence of food stains and holes all over their sweaters—spilled out of the classroom, resulting in the brothers quickly hurling themselves behind the tottering door, hoping none of the fleeing children had spotted them in their haste to get out.

"What are you three doing hiding behind there? I don't remember seeing you before," said a shocked looking boy who was wearing a grubby, creased T-shirt and a pair of threadbare trousers held up by a frayed piece of string. The washed out wording across the front of the T-shirt was anybody's guess.

Their first instincts were to run away as fast as possible, but their legs had suddenly become paralyzed.

It was Jordan who eventually broke the uneasy silence.

"I might ask you that same question, *boy*," snapped Jordan with some venom, trying very hard to sound brave, especially under the frightening circumstances they'd found themselves in.

Taken aback by Jordan's confident reply, the boy composed himself before answering. "Well, if you must know, my name's Scally, and that horrible group down there is called the Scallywags, and *we* all live here. So do *you* have any more questions, *boy*?"

The three of them began to shuffle around; with Jordan and Thomas quickly coming to the conclusion that James had been correct all along that there was something not right about this place.

Once again, it was Jordan who took the initiative.

"Oh! We're just visiting our aunt and uncle for a few days," stammered Jordan, his face a mask of terror. Warning bells were beginning to ring inside his head.

"Hey, you lot, just stop where you are, and take a look at what we've got back here," barked Scally to the Scallywags, who were by now halfway down the corridor. "It seems as though Mr. Bones and Miss Bones have relatives staying at the hall. Quick! One of you go and find Sir and tell him what we've found, and in the meantime, we'll make these three welcome," chuckled Scally, slightly menacingly.

"I've got a nasty feeling about all of this," muttered Thomas under his breath, the hairs on the back of his neck beginning to rise.

"I guess *now's* the time for us to leave, Jordan. I think we've overstayed our welcome, don't you think?" whimpered James from out of the corner of his mouth.

Jordan and Thomas nodded their heads in agreement, all three slinking away from the horrid, dirty, smelly boy.

"Go . . . go . . . go!" bellowed Jordan, elbowing Scally to one side, giving them a big enough gap to make their escape.

## Chapter Nine

When Jordan shouted "go," he'd expected all three to head off in the same direction. Unfortunately—that wasn't the case. Jordan barged past Scally and bolted toward the front door, where to his horror he saw that the dirty looking children had blocked it off. In his haste, he slipped and fell with a jarring crash, landing heavily up against the wall.

Thomas had set off to the back of the building, while James had rushed past Jordan and was well on his way down the corridor toward the slack-jawed children. Easing himself up on one knee and gazing down the corridor, Jordan saw, to his astonishment, James expertly raising his toes, resulting in the hidden wheels in the heels of his sneakers materializing. Craftily skating his way through the throng of bemused looking children, who at this stage were all staring at him in utter amazement at the unexpected display, James glided smoothly on his Heelys toward the foot of the stairs, giggling to himself at his own dazzling freaky spectacle.

"Oh sh . . . sugar!" shrieked Jordan, wondering what

to do next.

Quickly coming to the conclusion that his two younger brothers weren't heading in the same direction, Jordan steadied himself before pushing Scally to one side and dashing to where Thomas was headed, praying that James would be able to find a way of escaping out of the hall without his help. Tears were starting to trickle down his dirt-smudged cheeks.

Realizing he had no way of being able to get back to join Jordan and Thomas, James decided to try and find a way out of the building by clambering up the long, winding staircase, hoping to escape out of a bedroom window and climb down a drainpipe to freedom.

Arriving by Thomas's side, who by now was frozen to the spot, staring at the unbelievable scene unfolding before him, Jordan hastily grabbed hold of him by the hand and dragged him unceremoniously toward the first room they came across, which was the kitchen. He hoped it would lead them out of the hall.

Before closing and locking the door to the kitchen, Jordan glanced back down the corridor, only to catch sight of James scrambling up the stairs. Jordan was finding it difficult to hold down a lump in his throat, knowing full well that it was his entire fault they had ended up in this unbelievable nightmare.

Meanwhile, James was frantically climbing up the winding stairs on his hands and knees. He was gradually beginning to run out of breath, and sweat was starting to trickle down into his eyes, making them sting. And to make matters worse, the roughly laid stair carpet was causing him to lose his footing a number of times in his haste to reach the safety of the landing.

Finding himself at the top of the stairs, James stopped to take in his surroundings, quickly detecting small beams of light spreading out from beneath a number of doors down the dark corridor up ahead.

*Great!* he thought. To James it meant just one thing—a means of escape. He suddenly became worried, not knowing if any of the children had had an opportunity to go and warn "Sir," and also wondering if Sir was skulking about in one of the rooms up ahead.

At that moment, downstairs in the gloomy hall, the small group of children—who were still blocking the path to the front door—had recovered from the shock of seeing James hovering before their eyes. They quickly broke off into two groups; one group scampered down the corridor after Jordan and Thomas, while the other quickly bounded up the winding staircase, hoping to seize James, who by now was hastily making his way down the dingy corridor, all the while rubbing the stitch in his side.

Safely reaching the first room that had a beam of light spreading out from the bottom of the door; the sound of his heart pounding in his ears, he leaned against the wall and turned his head to gaze back down the corridor. To his alarm, he observed a number of sinister, elongated shadows dancing along the sides of the walls, aware that they were the children who were rapidly making their way up the long winding stairs—to get to him. Not wanting to be seen by the pursuing children, he reached out for the door handle and turned it. To his horror, the door didn't budge one little bit; it was stuck. James was now beginning to panic as he could hear the sounds of running feet on the stairs. He desperately turned the handle backward and forward one more time, but again with no success. With a quick jerk of his head toward the top of the stairs, he could make out the swaying silhouettes of the children reflected on the walls and ceiling.

"Great, that's all I need!" he gasped, wiping the buildup of sweat from the palms of his hands on his sleeves.

As he was frantically struggling for the third time with the door handle, his knuckles brushed up against a key, which had been left in the lock. In a flash, he quickly turned it, and to his relief the door yawned open. He sneakily slipped inside and pushed the door shut behind him; yet he wasn't too confident that the children had spotted him disappear into the room.

"Never mind," he grumbled under his breath, firmly shutting the door behind him, hastily locking it. He decided to leave the key in the lock, and rotated it a few millimeters. This way, he thought, it may prevent anyone on the outside from entering the room by using a spare key. He then kept perfectly still, not daring to breathe or move a muscle, aware that someone, or something, was lurking very, very close, and only a few inches from the seat of his pants. He could feel the hairs on his arms and the back of his neck stand up; his mouth became dry. It suddenly occurred to him that there could be only one reason why a door would be securely locked from the outside . . .

Someone doesn't want whoever's inside the room . . . to get out!

## Chapter Ten

While the filthy children outside in the corridor were trying to force open the locked kitchen door, Jordan and Thomas were desperately searching on the other side for a way out of the kitchen; the look of disappointment engrained on both their faces when they'd spotted the door leading out to the back of the building had wooden planks nailed across the width of the door, preventing them from opening it.

Quickly examining the gloomy room, Jordan—much to his relief—spotted a small opening in the corner of the room, and quickly figured out it was an elevator.

"Thomas, go over there. I'm going to send you upstairs in that elevator."

"Don't be so stupid, Jordan. That's not an elevator; it's far too small," said Thomas, following Jordan's gaze.

"It's called a dumbwaiter. They used them in the olden days to send meals to the other rooms in the house, rather than having the servants carry large heavy trays up and down the stairs," replied Jordan, ushering Thomas over to the dumbwaiter with a gentle nudge.

"Lazybones," mumbled Thomas under his breath.

"Come on, Tom, we haven't got time to mess around," responded Jordan, listening out for any movement outside in the corridor, as it had become eerily quiet.

"What are you going to do, Jordan? There won't be enough time for us both to escape before the children find a way of getting in here!" cried Thomas, aware that his big brother may be caught.

"Don't concern yourself about me, it's you and James I'm worried about . . . I'll be fine," answered Jordan, and wishing he were back in the tent, curled up in his sleeping bag.

While Jordan and Thomas were frantically searching for a way out of the kitchen, the filthy children out in the corridor had managed to collect a chair from one of the classrooms, and they were now in the process of smashing in the kitchen door. From the bulges and cracks appearing in the wooden paneling, Jordan knew he didn't have much time to send Thomas up to the next floor. Thomas was just about to pull his legs and hands inside the dumbwaiter, when there came an almighty snapping sound from the direction of the door, leaving a line of pale, dusty beams lancing through the shattered door.

Twisting his head around, Thomas noticed dozens of dirty hands stretching through the gaps in the splintered wooden paneling of the door, immediately reminding him of snakes having been woken up from a deep, deep sleep.

"Hurry up, Jordan, they'll be on to us soon!" screamed Thomas, panicking, his eyes bugging wide.

The inside of the elevator was dirty and smelled damp. Tom quickly folded his legs in and bent his head forward.

Jordan didn't need to know what was happening behind him, as he could see the children's groping hands reaching through the door in an old polished copper pot hanging on a hook inside a large stone fireplace over to his right.

"Hold on tight, Tom, and make sure your hands and feet are tucked well inside, and I'll see you soon," said Jordan, pulling on the ropes. With a little jolt and some shaking, the dumbwaiter began to move inside the shaft. But not upward as they had expected–but down . . . to the cellar . . .

"Oh no . . . Jordan? The elevator's going down, not up. You know I don't like dark smelly cellars, Jorda-a-a-a . . . !" The sound of Thomas's distraught voice faded away into the dark damp depths of the hall.

"Thomas, Thomas, can you hear me?" yelled Jordan as he leaned over the side of the elevator shaft. "When you reach the bottom, climb out and wait for me. I'll try and get down to you as soon as I can. Tom, Tom, can you hear me? Tom . . . Tom . . .?" Jordan lowered himself to the ground and began to cry; aware of what Thomas was going through, as he also hated dark enclosed places.

As he was feeling guilty for putting his two brothers in so much danger, Jordan watched the kitchen door come off its hinges, followed by a crazy mob of children barging their way inside, fanning around the room, ensuring he had no way of escaping—again.

Luckily, Thomas had heard Jordan's frantic instructions. So once he was safely at the bottom of the elevator shaft, he cautiously climbed out. Adjusting his eyes to the dark interior, he decided to stay close to the elevator for a while, as it was giving him a small amount of light to see. He was just about to be brave and start to explore the room when he heard the creaking sounds of the elevator rising back up to the kitchen.

"Uh oh," mumbled Thomas, his eyes darting manically as he tried to pick objects out of the gloom of the room, hoping to find something that may stop the dumbwaiter from moving and preventing anyone from coming down—to get him.

Due to his gloomy surroundings, he couldn't make out too much. Gingerly shuffling his feet and reaching out with his small hands, he began to blindly feel his way through the darkness, probing for any kind of tool he might be able to use. He had only moved a short distance when his trembling fingers made contact with something cold and metallic, resulting in a tinkling sound echoing all around the cellar. Relieved that he may have found something he could use, he hastily unhooked what looked like to him like an old brass two-pronged fork and a long thick wooden spoon.

Making it safely back to the opening of the shaft, he noticed, to his alarm, that the small elevator had almost reached the kitchen. *Now what do I do with these?* he thought, examining the two utensils in his hands. Craning his neck and peering up into the dusty gloom of the shaft, he spied two sets of ropes suspended on either side. He knew immediately that they were the means of operating the elevator. With that thought in mind, he hastily wedged the prongs of the fork between the ropes into one side of the wooden framework of the elevator, and with the spoon, he intertwined the loose dangling ropes around it before jamming it inside a crack on the other side. He then stood back to inspect his handiwork, hoping that his quick thinking might deter anyone from using the elevator.

Suddenly, there was a loud creaking sound. The ropes began to shudder and groan under the weight of someone inside the elevator's cramped compartment. Slowly, it started to descend toward him. He stood there trying to stay calm, biting the inside of his lip to keep from screaming out. A few tense and frightening seconds later, the elevator jolted to a shuddering halt, much to Thomas's delight.

"That was pretty smart," he cried, jumping up and down on the spot, knowing that his quick thinking had worked.

"We know where you are, little boy, and once we have the three of you safely locked away, you'll be so-r-r-y!" came the manic echoing voice from above, combined with the sound of someone strenuously attempting to crawl out of the elevator.

Thomas collapsed onto the cold stone floor and shut his eyes against the burn of tears, worrying for his brothers who were trapped somewhere upstairs. He missed his brothers like crazy.

## Chapter Eleven

James stood rooted to the spot, wondering what on earth was creeping behind him. Eventually, he found the courage to move. He let out a breath he'd been holding and gritted his teeth before cautiously turning his head around, slowly glancing down. To his revulsion, leering up at him were three large black Doberman dogs, drooling long strings of saliva out of the corners of their mouths onto the threadbare carpet. He felt his scalp begin to prickle and his legs tremble. Keeping as still as possible—he didn't want to spook the dogs—he began to survey his surroundings, searching for a way of out of this horrible nightmare.

The room was filled with tired looking wooden furniture; most of it seemed to be coated in a thin layer of dust. The wall to his right had a huge stone fireplace. Flames were leaping up the chimney and throwing red shadows across the flagstone floor, giving off some welcoming light for him to see. Positioned in one corner was an old grandfather clock, its winding mechanism beginning to come to life, the Westminster chimes striking one o'clock, which suddenly brought

James out of his waking nightmare.

He desperately rummaged through his coat pockets for the biscuits he'd sneakily slipped inside before leaving the lodge. "Yes!" he whispered in delight, as his trembling fingers made contact with a number of broken pieces of biscuits that had been mixed in with an assortment of other items he kept in his pockets.

Bending over slightly, he tentatively offered the biscuits to the three dogs, ensuring his fingers weren't too close to their powerful, slavering jaws. As the three dogs slowly advanced toward him, he scattered the biscuits on the saliva-stained carpet, hoping the dogs would take the bait long enough for him to sidle across to the window and—hopefully—freedom.

He was just about to inch away from the dogs when he heard the sounds of doors being opened and slammed shut down the corridor. He instantly knew that the children were in the process of searching all of the upstairs rooms for him. With that dreadful thought in mind, he quickly scanned the room for somewhere to hide, his gaze settling on a large wooden sea chest positioned at the foot of an enormous four-poster bed. Now that the dogs were busy licking the biscuits up from the floor, James cunningly made his way over to the chest and lifted the lid, only to notice, to his disappointment, that the inside was stuffed full of blankets and what looked like an assortment of old, wrinkled, smelly clothes. Knowing that he didn't have any time to look for anywhere else to hide, he quickly grabbed ahold of as many items as he could carry in his small hands and flung them underneath the bed, ensuring that none of them were sticking out so no one would spot them when entering the room. He had just finished pulling out a heap of blankets when he heard voices and the sound of heavy footfalls coming down the corridor—and growing stronger.

Seconds later, those footsteps reached outside his room, and then they stopped. Certain that the dogs were too busy to notice where he was about to hide, he carefully wrapped a blanket around his head and shoulders, before slowly climbing into the chest and closing the lid. The smell coming from the inside was revolting.

"This smell reminds me of old people," he mumbled to himself, pinching his nose with the tips of his fingers. Suddenly, he was brought out of his worried thoughts by the frenzied rattling sounds of the door handle. Someone was desperately trying to enter the room.

"Unlock this door this minute, boy," demanded the male voice coming from outside in the corridor. "We know you're in there; we're not going to harm you, are we, Grace?"

"No, heaven forbid, we just lo-o-o-v-e children," replied a woman's piercing hysterical voice.

James was trying hard to tuck himself further down inside the trunk, but there was so little room. He was just beginning to feel confident when there was an almighty ear-splitting noise. He was now scared, *very* scared, wondering what would become of him, when they eventually found him.

"We know you're in here, little boy, and don't even think about escaping, for there is *no* escape from Thorngarth Hall. So show yourself and then we can have a cozy little chat. What do you say?" called out the old man, steadying himself on the doorframe before stretching his long legs out over the damaged horizontal bedroom door.

Squeezing himself further down toward the bottom of the chest, James covered his head and shoulders with another smelly blanket, praying that they wouldn't spot him if they did open the lid of the chest to check inside. He felt that even breathing too loudly would give him away. His heart thudded against his chest, and to his disgust, he heard a scrabbling noise, very close to his ear, which caused him to hold his breath and his skin to crawl.

"Oh no, what's that?" he whimpered, shaking with fear, conscious of the fact he may have disturbed something nasty in the smelly chest. He was now finding it difficult to breathe from having his head buried deep inside the blanket. Rivulets of sweat rolled down his forehead, which he brushed away with the tips of his fingers.

Keeping as still as possible, the sound of his own breathing echoing around the enclosed space, he scrunched his eyes tightly shut and began to think nice thoughts. To his pleasant surprise, the back of his shaking hand brushed up against a small furry creature, which James instantly knew was a small mouse. Very delicately, he wrapped his small fingers around the shivering rodent before lifting up his sweater, carefully placing the mouse inside the folds of his shirt. He was being cautious, as he didn't want to smother the mouse.

"You'll be much safer in there, little one," he whispered, stroking the small bulge evident on his stomach. Sensing it wasn't going to be harmed in any way, the mouse began to slowly circle around the inside of James's shirt, snuggling down between the folds and creases, feeling both safe and warm. To James's surprise, the mouse began to knead its tiny-clawed feet into his sweaty skin, tickling him, causing him to cry out in alarm and bang his head on the lid of the chest.

"A-a-a-a-a-h!" he yelled, as he erupted from the wooden sea chest like a Jack-in-the-Box, surprising his pursuers, who were all scouring the room, searching for him.

"Well, well, well, what do we have here, Grace?" asked the old man, peering over the top of his gold, wire-framed glasses.

"Two down, two to go," answered the old woman, smirking. "Come on, Mr. Bones, let's take him upstairs to the attic. There's still six hours before sunrise. Isn't it bizarre? We don't have any visitors for four years, and then in the space of a few minutes, we have four new faces . . . interesting," she continued, leering over at James with the meanest eyes James had ever seen, causing him to shiver.

Once he'd calmed himself down, James shuffled his feet around at the bottom of the chest to keep his balance, while staring at the old man and woman as they both headed his way. James couldn't believe his eyes. They were almost identical. They were tall and slim, at least seven feet, he guessed. Both wore gold, wire-rimmed glasses perched on the end of their long pointy noses. The woman had long, straggly white hair, which hung loosely down the sides of her face, making her resemble a weather-beaten old scarecrow. The old man had a ruddy complexion, topped with thick, bushy eyebrows. He had long white hair, raked back into a tightly-bound pony tail, and to James's amusement, he had a pointy white beard, which the old man kept on stroking as he made his way over toward him.

"Weirdos," James whispered under his breath, shaking his head. He also observed that they were both wearing the same old-fashioned clothes; the only difference was that she had a herringbone dress that matched her loose-fitting coat, which covered a white lacy blouse. The old man had a pair of flared herringbone trousers that matched his double-breasted frock coat that concealed a hideous looking checkered shirt and waistcoat. Both coats, James noticed, had leather patches crudely sewn onto the elbows.

"I'll have to stop reading those creepy horror novels in future," mumbled James, thinking that the next time he came across Jordan, he'd thump him for getting him into this mess.

The old man strode across the room, stroking his goatee beard, and carefully lifted James out of the chest, gripping him by both arms, preventing him from escaping. At this stage, James had accepted his fate and was waiting for Jordan and Thomas to appear. *Hopefully they can work out a plan of escaping from here,* he thought. He then quickly clamped his lips to stop him from crying out with laughter, as he could see the three dogs scouring the floor in search of more biscuits.

"Some guard dogs they turned out to be," he chuckled under his breath, "And what was that all about? Six hours to sunrise, and four new faces. There are only three of us. Can't she count? The silly old bat," he snickered, struggling to pull aside the smelly blanket from around his shoulders.

"What was that you said, young man?" snapped the old woman, her eyes burning into his brain.

"Nothing for nosy parkers," replied James, lowering his gaze, wondering what Jordan and Thomas were up to.

## Chapter Twelve

It didn't take long for Jordan to come to the conclusion that he had no way of making a run for it from the dirty children who had circled him in the kitchen. He just hoped and prayed that James had managed to find a way out of the hall, and Thomas was safe down in the cellar. After hearing Scally calling down the elevator shaft to Thomas, he did have the satisfaction of knowing that Thomas had somehow managed to find a way of deterring the children from going down after him, which made Jordan smile.

Roughly hoisting Jordan up off the floor by both of his arms, Scally and the rest of the children escorted him through what was left of the doorway. Making sure he couldn't escape, they ushered Jordan down the long, dark corridor toward the large wooden staircase that would eventually take them upstairs to Mr. Bones and Miss Bones, the terrible twins.

While all this was going on in the hall, outside in the cold dark night, the snow was still falling heavily, causing the countless footprints they'd left in the snow to slowly fill in. If there was anyone out there searching for them, they wouldn't have any idea where to start.

Making their way down the gloomy corridor, Jordan began to study his surroundings. Glancing up to the high wooden ceiling, he noticed that it was supported by four long wooden beams, and suspended from them were hundreds of cobwebs. From where he was standing, he could make out thousands of spiders, all crawling around on any available space on the ceiling and between the wooden beams.

"Ugh!" he said to himself, turning away from the yucky site.

"What did you say, *boy*?" snapped Scally, glaring into Jordan's terrified, watery eyes.

"Nothing. I'm just talking to myself," replied Jordan, once again shuddering at the sight of all those spiders.

"Don't worry, *boy*, you'll have plenty of time to talk to yourself once you're inside the attic," remarked Scally, steering Jordan by the elbow toward the bottom of the stairs.

When they had reached the top of the long winding staircase, Jordan was shocked to see dozens of rooms down the long corridor as far as the eye could see.

"The hall seems to be larger inside than from the outside," he whispered to himself, grimly "Is this some weird nightmare I've found myself in?"

Swiftly making their way down the long corridor, Jordan—much to his relief—heard James's voice coming from within one of the rooms where a glimmer of light shone through the open doorway.

"Thank goodness, he's safe," he muttered to himself, his eyes beginning to mist over.

Seconds later, James appeared from out of one of the rooms, and being held tightly by two tall, identical-looking, weird, old people. They both looked so pale and thin that they seemed luminous in the faint light coming from behind. He also noted that they had to stoop down so they could pass through the doorway without banging their heads.

*Oh crap!* thought Jordan. *What have I gotten myself into now?*

"Jordan!" called out James, spotting his older brother. James began to struggle, trying desperately to get away from their tight grips, wanting to be by the side of his older brother, tears beginning to form in his eyes.

"Let him go! And don't hurt him, you big ugly bullies!" called out Jordan, once again astounded by the appearance of the two adults, wondering if there was a mirror hung up on the wall reflecting only one person.

"Now, now, then, we don't have naughty boys in this house, do we children?" declared the old woman, snickering behind her bony hand, smiling wickedly.

"No, Miss Bones," echoed the dirty looking children.

It was then when Jordan accepted the fact that there were actually two people standing in front of him and not just the one person, as both figures were so alike.

"This is something you read about in horror books.

I must be dreaming," he mumbled to himself, feeling totally downhearted.

"Where's the other boy, Scally?" yelled the old man, peering over the top of his glasses.

"Don't you worry about him, sir. He's down in the dark, damp cellar. There's no way out of there, apart from the dumbwaiter, and I can't imagine him forcing open the locked cellar door, sir. When he becomes cold and hungry, he'll soon make his way back up to the kitchen or shout up to us to be let out. That's when we'll be ready and waiting for him. We'll pop down in a few minutes, once these two are safely locked away," answered Scally, glaring menacingly at Jordan and James.

"Come on, let's not be hanging around here all night. We need to take these two upstairs to the attic. And after the sun's risen sufficiently, you can let them all out and give them something to eat. We wouldn't want them to starve, now would we?" ordered the old man, the smile on his face giving the two brothers goose bumps. "Also, you'll need to catch up on your sleep." He gestured to the children with a sweep of his hand. "That's once we have the annoying little boy who's trapped down in the cellar. And Scally, make sure you are all awake and ready to keep guard on all of the exits at least one hour before the sun rises. We can't afford for any of these unwelcome guests to escape," he announced, once again staring over the top of his glasses at Jordan and James.

The brothers moved a little closer to each other for support, as they hadn't the foggiest idea what the old man was talking about, and they were both becoming concerned about Thomas, wondering what he was getting up to.

## Chapter Thirteen

Finally plucking up the courage to move around the gloomy cellar, Thomas stealthily slinked his way over toward the elevator, peering up into the dusty shaft, checking out what was happening one floor above. *Nothing, thank goodness,* he thought, edging away from the opening, once again thrilled that his timely actions had foiled the dirty children from coming down after him.

Feeling bolder, he decided to do some exploring, squinting into the inky darkness. After adjusting his eyes, he noticed that the cellar was filled to the high ceiling with cardboard boxes of varying shapes and sizes. There were dozens of them stacked down by the side of the walls and on wooden-slat shelving. He tentatively approached them, noting that they contained a variety of canned foods.

"It will just be my luck there won't be a blooming can opener down here," he mumbled under his breath, with a hint of a smile across his face.

As he was scanning the room, something caught his eye over by the far wall. Moving across and then crouching down on his hands and knees, he came across a large stone floor tile, which looked to have been made into a crudely constructed trap door. He also spotted a handle, which had been attached as a means of raising the trap door.

"A way out of this horrible place, I hope," he whispered to himself, his spirits now beginning to lift.

Steadying himself by positioning both legs firmly apart, he securely gripped the handle with both hands, and somehow managed to ease open the trap door a few inches. To his disgust, the stench, which had been trapped deep beneath the depths of the hall for decades, came drifting out of the gaping hole.

"That's revolting!" he cried, quickly taking a step back from the awful sour smell, which was escaping through the dark hole. "It's disgusting. I don't fancy climbing down there . . . but I suppose I've no choice in the matter. I wouldn't dare risk climbing up the elevator shaft," said a worried Thomas, his senses slowly beginning to get used to the aroma that was floating around the cramped room.

Once composed, he slid the trapdoor a few more inches to one side of the opening and began to search around the room, hoping to find some candles, and more importantly, matches.

He was being extra careful, as he could only see a few feet in front of him. Slowly edging his way over toward the opening of the elevator, he came across a wooden chest of drawers. Knowing he couldn't see too much, he used his hands to feel around the front, searching for a handle.

"Yes! Found one. Now let's see what's hidden inside," he mumbled to himself, opening the drawer. Aware that he may cut himself if there were any sharp objects or razorblades hidden deep inside, he carefully rummaged around with his small trembling fingers, pushing to one side any objects that didn't feel like they could be candles. A few tense seconds later, his left hand brushed away a small tubular object, which ended up rolling toward the back of the drawer. Thomas knew instantly it was a candle. As he was cautiously probing with his hands near the back of the drawer, he felt a spider scurrying across the back of his hand, which no doubt Thomas had woken up from a deep sleep.

"M-U-M!" he screamed out, quickly ramming his hand under his armpit to wipe away any remnants of fur or legs that may have ended up there. Having got his breathing back to normal, he jerked his hand back into the drawer, quickly grabbing hold of the candle, and ramming the drawer shut with an almighty crash.

"Phew, I wasn't expecting that," croaked Thomas, knowing the spider was probably more scared of him. He then started to guide his hands over to the other end of the chest, hoping to find another drawer, and more importantly, some matches. *I can't imagine anyone storing candles down here without matches,* he thought, despairingly.

"Great, another drawer," he cried. Not wanting to disturb any more creepy-crawlies, he decided to use the candle as a way of sweeping any objects stored inside to one side, praying he would hear the familiar rattling sounds of matches. Seconds later, the candle struck something, which to Thomas's sensitive ears, sounded very much like it could be what he was searching for. Swiftly reaching inside, grabbing the first thing his hand touched, he happily pulled out a large box of matches.

"Great," he cried, checking its contents. Satisfied that the box contained some matches, he picked up a small glass jar from the top of the chest, safely placing the candle inside.

"I do hope Jordan and James are safe," sobbed Thomas, now feeling lonely and cold in the gloomy cellar.

## Chapter Fourteen

While the dirty children and the two creepy adults closely guarded them up the long winding staircase to the attic, James decided to stop and inspect a number of black and white photographs hanging on both sides of the walls. He then recalled the ones downstairs in the corridor that he'd seen when they had first arrived.

"Jordan, back in the olden days, was it just black and white? Didn't they have any colors then?" asked James, his eyes flicking from one picture to another.

"What do you mean by that?" replied Jordan, a look of confusion on his face.

"Well, as far as I can tell, all the pictures I've seen in this place are in black and white," answered James, glancing up at Jordan.

"Don't be so dumb; they didn't have cameras with colored film in those days," replied Jordan, smiling and ruffling James's hair.

"Oh, thanks for that, Jordan. Silly me," giggled James, smoothing down his hair with the palm of his hand.

"James, what did the old man mean when he told

Scally to be alert and to guard all the exits to the hall one hour before the sun rises?" inquired Jordan, licking his dry lips.

"I've got no idea, Jordan. Nothing will surprise me about this place," commented James. "Why don't you go over and ask him? We can't get into anymore trouble than we are already in," he suggested, nudging Jordan gently over toward the old man.

"Mister, what's going to happen when the sun rises?" inquired Jordan, tugging at the man's coat sleeve.

"There's no way of you escaping now, so I will tell you. Do you know what day it is today?" questioned the old man, plucking his glasses off from the end of his nose and wiping them with a red silk handkerchief he'd produced from his breast coat pocket.

"The twenty-ninth of February, 2008. It's a leap year. Leap years come around every four years," answered Jordan with confidence.

"Yes, that's correct, you annoying little boy. And if you don't discover the way of getting out of the hall before the sun rises, you and the rest of your meddlesome little group will be stuck in here with us for another four years before you have the next opportunity of escaping," roared the old man, slipping his glasses back on his nose, and staring down into Jordan and James's terrified looking faces.

"Jordan what does he mean? I don't like the sound of that!" cried a nervous and frightened James. "I knew it would be a bad idea coming here with you tonight," he said, punching Jordan hard on the arm.

"I haven't got the faintest idea, James; let's just wait and see what happens to us once we're in the attic, and then we can sit down and try to think of a way of getting out of here," commented Jordan, rubbing his throbbing arm and once again wishing he was back home, fast asleep.

The two brothers became silent as they were herded up the long, winding narrow stair-case and along the low-ceilinged dusky corridors, which unfortunately for them was taking them further away from the front door of the hall—and freedom.

As they were being shepherded from one landing to another, Jordan couldn't help but notice a series of passages and landings, all going off in different directions. He suddenly became concerned. If they did manage to escape from the "attic," it may be difficult to remember where all the passages led.

Nearing the top of the tall building, James paused, as he could hear rustling and scraping above him in the loft. "I wonder what that is. It's probably just the wind," he told himself, before moving on, but only after being prodded from behind by Scally.

Minutes later, they reached the top of the steep staircase; the old man raised his hand, signaling for the children to stop where they were. From out of his coat pocket, he produced a long, thick brass chain, on which a bunch of brass keys hung loosely from the end.

Once he had unlocked the door, the old man slowly eased it open, before groping around with his right hand on the wall. Eventually finding the light switch, he turned it on.

The two boys entered a narrow room, and from the low ceiling hung a single flickering lightbulb dangling from a dusty flex of cable. The floor seemed to be covered in a half-inch layer of dust, and placed down one side were four old brass beds. To the boys' astonishment, curled up inside two of them were two children, with tousled hair and bleary eyes as if they'd been roused from sleep. And peering over the bedclothes of the bed positioned at the far corner of the room was a skulking boy wearing a baseball cap. He was staring fearfully back at them in a total state of bewilderment.

"Billy Three Ha-Ha . . . happy to see you, Billy!" gasped Jordan, his face glazed over with shock.

"Quiet!" shouted the old woman, stamping her feet on the wooden floor for added emphasis.

The old woman pushed Jordan and James into the center of the dusty room. The brothers were finding it hard to tear their eyes away from Billy and the two cowering children.

"Go back to sleep, you three; it isn't time to get up yet, and we've brought some new friends to keep you company," called out the old man, forcefully guiding Jordan and James well away from the entrance. The old man then quickly turned around, stepping back into the gloomy corridor and closing the door behind him, securely locking it.

The two brothers stood on the spot like statues, not knowing what to say or do. James shuffled his feet toward Jordan, seizing ahold of his hand for some means of support.

Now that they were alone and feeling relatively safe, Billy swung his legs over the edge of the bed and ran over to the two brothers, tears streaming down his face, his whole body shaking with joy.

"Am I glad to see you two! It's really spooky, especially with those two, who haven't said a word since I've been stuck in here," said Billy, glaring over his shoulder at the two children who were still huddled beneath their bedclothes. "And aren't those two old weirdos creepy?" he questioned, wiping away the tears with the back of his hand.

"Billy, how come you're in here?" inquired Jordan, once he'd gotten his composure back. Jordan didn't raise the issue about the other two children, as he already had a fair idea who they were. He decided it would be best if he kept those scary facts to himself for the time being.

"Let's go and sit down over there, then I can tell you everything that's happened to me," suggested Billy, guiding them over to one of the beds.

Satisfied he had their undivided attention, Billy propped himself up with a pillow at the top of the bed, and started to describe his nightmarish ordeal.

## Chapter Fifteen

"Jordan? I've a confession to make . . . I've been keeping a watchful eye on you for most of the day, checking out whether you were going to be brave enough to take on my dare . . . I followed you down to the lodge this afternoon. And when I spotted you with the rolled up blankets tucked under your arm, along with the bulging plastic shopping bag, I knew you were going to go ahead with the dare." Billy paused to get his thoughts back into some semblance of order before carrying on. "I sneaked over to your house this evening, and I've been drifting around down the road, waiting for you. I was freezing. Have you any idea how cold it is hanging around in this cold weather? Now where was I? Oh, yes. When it began to snow heavily, I decided to take cover in a porch just two doors up from your house. I'm surprised none of you spotted me, as you were making your way up the road. At one point, I had to crawl over a wall into a pile of yellow-looking snow. You were only a few feet from me when you passed by. You were so close; you could have shaken my hand," laughed Billy nervously, stopping once again, reliving his nightmare.

"When you reached the lodge, I decided to roam around the grounds of the hall. It was then I came across a rusty metal staircase fixed to the side of the building. I presumed it was the original fire escape. Anyway, I was freezing, so I started to jog around the grounds to keep myself warm. When I ended up back at the foot of the staircase, I glanced up toward the roof of the building. It was then I spotted an opening at the top, just where the stairs ended. I decided to climb up and investigate. I also knew it would be much warmer if I popped inside. I was being extra careful, as I wasn't too sure if the metal stairs were going to hold my weight. And to make matters worse, they were coated in a thin layer of ice, but I carried on anyway, like you do . . . I was concentrating so hard, making sure I wasn't going to slip and fall off, when I heard the sound of church bells striking midnight in the distance. Now I know you're not going to believe me. Within milliseconds of the twelfth strike, the hall suddenly returned back to how it is now, its original state. Now is that spooky or what?" asked Billy, waiting for some kind of response from one of them. But to his annoyance, he didn't get one from either of them, as Jordan and James were already aware of the transformation of the hall, along with its grounds.

Easing himself off the bed, turning around to face them both, Billy carried on with his story, and he was somewhat surprised he didn't get the reaction he was expecting.

"When I eventually reached the opening at the top of the building, it wasn't there anymore; it had been replaced by the original fire door. Luckily for me, it wasn't locked, so I carefully eased it open. I was only halfway through when, from out of the corner of my eye, I spotted a long bony hand reaching out to grab me. It grabbed me by the scruff of my shirt. The owner of the hand then hauled me unceremoniously inside. That's when I must have struck my head on something, and blacked out, because the next thing I remembered was just a few minutes before the door to this hovel opened up and you two came barging in. So now you know how I ended up in here, and while I'm at it, do either of you two have the foggiest idea how we're going to get out of this nightmare?" he asked, eyes darting from one brother to the other. "Also, where's your other brother, Tom?" he continued, anxiously waiting for an answer.

They all fell silent for a while. Jordan sat motionless on the bed, trying to gather his thoughts while peering across at James. Both of them were shaking their heads in total despair.

"I haven't the heart to tell you everything that's happened to us at this moment in time . . . but all I can say is that Thomas is somewhere all alone, down in the dark cellar of the hall. No doubt he'll be frightened and cold; he'll also be wondering what we're up to. Oh, and by the way, Billy, you might be interested to know: Those two adults you called old weirdos do have names. Don't laugh; they're called Mr. Bones and Miss Bones. There's also a group of dirty kids living here too called the Scallywags, and they have a kid called Scally who seems to be in charge," said Jordan, lifting himself off the bed, his mind in turmoil.

"No way. You've got to be kidding me, Waldron. They only have creepy names like that in horror books . . . don't they?" asked Billy, staring across at Jordan. "Is it true, James?" inquired Billy, waiting for James to start giggling, assuming Jordan was only pulling his leg.

"Sure is; those are their names, Billy," answered James, shaking with fright, as it was now dawning on him that they were all in some deep, serious trouble . . .

Jordan began to pace the floor, concentrating hard, trying to figure out a way of getting out of this awful mess he had landed them in. He just hoped and prayed Thomas had somehow found a way of getting out of the cellar, safely.

## Chapter Sixteen

After slamming the drawer shut, Thomas hesitantly selected a match from the box and struck it, hoping it wasn't too damp to ignite. Unfortunately, the small lump of phosphorous on the end broke up into tiny pieces.

"Oh poo," he groaned, fumbling around in the box for another match. Closely examining the tips of the remaining matches, he came up with one that felt dry to the touch. Then, holding it as close to the tip as possible, so as not to break it or burn his trembling fingers, he struck the match. After the second attempt, it flared up, giving Thomas some additional light. He lit the wick of the candle, dripped hot wax into the jar, and then pressed the candle against it to hold it in place. The light from the candle was giving out a small halo that reflected in the odd objects that were dotted around the dreary cellar.

Confident that the flame wouldn't blow out, he began to investigate the rest of the room, hoping he may come across some more candles that may have been stored away on any of the old dusty shelves. Or, if he was really lucky, a flashlight. He was now feeling more cheerful.

Some minutes later, after rummaging around all the cluttered dusty shelves and cupboards, he thankfully came up with two additional candles, plus an old oil lamp, which had a small amount of grungy looking oil floating around at the bottom of its glass base. He decided it would be best not to light the lamp, as he might accidentally knock it over and cause a fire, which was the last thing he wanted.

Now having some means of seeing where he was going, he decided to explore beneath the trapdoor, praying it may be a way out of the hall, knowing that it would be dark, cold, and frightening down there.

Surveying the dark gloomy room, he caught a glimpse of a door that had been partly hidden behind a stack of cardboard boxes. Aware he may have found a way out of this smelly and unpleasant cellar, he decided to go over and check it out. Noticing that there wasn't a handle on his side of the door, he shrugged his shoulders, made a face, and stepped away.

Heading back across the stone-tiled floor to the trapdoor, the reflection coming from the candle in the glass jar was making it difficult for him to see where he was putting his feet, and he ended up with the tips of his wet sneakers precariously hanging over the edge of the gaping hole. Quickly realizing the dangerous predicament he was in, he nimbly backed away from the opening. He somehow collided with a large heavy wooden table, which caused him to bounce back toward the opening, with him ending up teetering on the edge of the hole, his arms wind-milling frantically. Eventually he managed to regain his balance and pull himself back from the brink. For a heartbeat, Thomas stood where he was, realizing he could have fallen down the hole, and more than likely, seriously injured himself. He leaned against the wooden table, trying to control his breathing after his nasty scare.

To be on the safe side, he decided he would get down on his hands and knees and crawl toward the opening. Reaching the hole, he cautiously knelt down a few inches from the side, dropping a large screw—which he'd found on the floor by his knees —down into the bowels of the hall. It had only left his cold sweaty fingers a few seconds when he heard the distinctive metallic twang of the screw hitting the stone floor below.

"At least it doesn't seem to be a long way down . . . well, here goes," he mumbled to himself, the feeling of butterflies in the pit of his stomach.

Confident that the other candles and matches were safely tucked away in his coat pocket, he picked up his makeshift lantern and nervously perched himself on the edge of the dark imposing abyss, his legs dangling over the side. Taking a deep breath, he gingerly made his slow descent down the rusty wet ladders, which would ultimately plunge him down into the darkness.

Unbeknownst to him, he was entering the old rundown tunnel complex that had not been used for decades. And lurking down there in the filthy icy water were horrible dirty things, plus some unexpected surprises that Thomas wasn't going to like—not one little bit!

Slowly, and guardedly, he eventually reached the safety of the damp floor. Luckily, the flame from the candle was giving him sufficient light to see a few feet around him.

"What a stench! It smells as though something's crawled down here and died . . ." he suddenly stopped what he was saying, realizing what he had just said. "You don't have to frighten yourself, you silly boy, it's those creepy ones up there you have to be worried about," he whispered to himself, trying very hard to convince himself that he was far safer down here in the tunnel, instead of back up in the cellar. He was feeling frightened and lonely, and wondering what Jordan and James were getting up to.

## Chapter Seventeen

As soon as Billy had finished his exhaustive and frightening story, they all sat staring at one another.

After a moment of awkward silence, the three of them lifted themselves up from the bed, and made their way over to the two terrified children, scattering the dust on the floor around like flour on the way.

"H-h-h-ave you come to take us away from this beastly place?" mumbled the frail young girl, fear etched across her innocent looking face. "And what are your names, may I ask?"

After a few seconds, it was Jordan who eventually spoke up.

"My name's Jordan Waldron, and this is one of my younger brothers, James," he answered, pointing across at James. "We also have another brother with us; his name's Thomas, but at the moment we don't know where he is. The last time I saw him was when we were in the kitchen, and I sent him down toward the cellar in the dumbwaiter." Jordan paused to control his emotions, before carrying on. "Oh, and this is Billy

Three Ha-Ha . . . Billy, and I don't think you would believe me if I told you where we all came from. And what are your names?" he asked.

Realizing that the three boys weren't any kind of threat, the two children threw back their coarse blankets and leaped out of bed.

"My name's Amy Popple-Brownlow, and this is my younger brother Adam. Have you come to take us home?" she asked in a pleading voice.

"You're the two children who mysteriously went missing years ago, aren't you?" inquired Jordan, stepping away from James, waiting for some kind of reaction once the question had sunk into James's brain.

"You know all about us then?" cried Adam, clapping his hands, jumping up and down on the spot with joy.

"Yes, but I'm sorry, friends. At the moment we're all stuck in here. The only hope we have is if Thomas has somehow managed to find a way of escaping from the cellar and alerted someone. I'm just praying he hasn't been caught by that group up there," sniveled Jordan, trying very hard to hold down the lump that was forming in his throat.

"What's all this about kids disappearing years ago, Jordan?" questioned James, suddenly becoming scared once he'd fully grasped what Jordan had been saying.

At that stage, Jordan informed James about the chilling events surrounding the disappearance of the two children all those years ago. While all this was happening, Billy had moved a safe distance from the brothers as he was already aware of the missing children and it was his childish dare that put them in this horrible situation in the first place.

After digesting Jordan's pathetic confession, James stood still, his face a mask of terror.

"You've got to be kidding me, Jordan. If I'd known about this before, I would have thought twice before coming down to the lodge with you tonight. Does Thomas know about them?" asked an angry and upset James, a sickening wave of terror welling up from his belly.

"I don't think so, and don't you let on to him when we see him," said Jordan, hanging his head in shame, glancing down at his feet like a naughty schoolboy.

"Well you're a bigger bozo than I thought you were," shouted James, before moving across the room and collapsing onto one of the beds, his whole body shaking with rage.

Feeling guilty about putting his brothers in so much danger, Jordan made his way over toward James, plunking himself down and snuggling up to him.

"I'm sorry, James; I didn't think anything awful would happen to us tonight. And the stories about the missing kids—well, I thought they were made up by the grown-ups, to stop children like us from entering the grounds and the hall." His voice was now beginning to break up.

James had been crying throughout Jordan's pitiful

apology, causing Jordan to start sniffling.

"Come on, James, we can't be hanging around here all night; we need to find a way out of this mess, and more importantly, we need to find Tom, and soon," muttered Jordan, his voice hardly more than a whisper. Jordan then glanced up to see the other three wandering over.

"The old man mentioned we'd be stuck in here for four years if we don't discover the way out of the hall before sun up," said Jordan, gazing over at Amy and Adam. "Is that true?"

"Yes . . . when the sun rises, the hall, plus the surrounding buildings and grounds, reverts back to its old decrepit state for another four years . . . the next leap year!" sobbed Amy, wiping away the tears with the back of her hand.

"Oh crap!" cried James. "What are we going to do now? Jordan, what time is it? If I remember correctly, the sun comes up around 7 a.m. this time of year."

Jordan checked the time on his watch. "Two a.m. . . . that means we have, at the most, five hours to find a way of getting out of this place; if not, we're going to be stuck in here for four years, and I certainly have no intentions of that happening to any of us," exclaimed Jordan, panic evident in his voice, once again wondering what Thomas was getting up to.

## Chapter Eighteen

Moving like a shadow down the narrow tunnel, trying to avoid walking in the river of stagnant water that was slowly running down the center, Thomas suddenly halted, as he could hear something directly behind him that sounded very much like scurrying little feet, combined with the echoing sounds of splashing and squeaking. Thomas had a fair idea who the owners of those feet were: rats!

Not wanting to be bowled over by the rats, he quickly searched for somewhere to climb up onto, spying an alcove a few feet over to his right with a small ledge jutting out.

He hastily stepped across the putrid water, which was now swarming with dozens of scampering rats, and hoisted himself up onto the ledge, instantly feeling its ice-cold surface through the seat of his jeans. Having gotten over the initial shock, he gazed down; only to see a multitude of filthy long-tailed rats high-tailing down the dark tunnel, creating the illusion of a rippling, dirty grey carpet.

"I wonder what spooked them?" he asked himself

as the last of the rats passed by a few inches from his dangling wet sneakers.

Convinced that there was no likelihood of anymore rats appearing, he carefully pushed himself off from the ledge and carried on down the tunnel, stopping now and again to check out the other network of passageways, wondering whether to follow a different path or not. He decided to follow the direction of the rats, hoping they may lead him out to freedom.

Every now and again, he'd sneak a glance at the small flame of the candle as he navigated his way through the tunnels, wishing it would flutter; then at least he would know there was a draft coming from somewhere up ahead. It suddenly felt eerily quiet, which made his skin crawl, and he noticed moisture flowing down the side of the walls that glowed in the dark from the flickering flame of the candle.

Hugging the curve of the wall, he moved deeper and deeper into the dark unwelcoming tunnels, peering down at his reflection in the stagnant water passing by his wet sneakers. Hundreds of cobwebs hung down from the roof, which he swiped away with his cold hand. The temperature seemed to be getting colder by the second. With his collar pulled up and his jacket tightly zipped up to his neck, he plodded on regardless, concentrating hard on where he was putting his feet.

After a few tentative strides, he spotted something lying by the foot of the wall. He decided to go over and investigate (like most boys would), and warily nudged the object with the toe cap of his filthy wet sneakers. To his disgust, it was the remains of a large furry animal. Must have been what that horrible smell was coming from, he assumed, moving away, as he was now starting to feel sick from the sight.

Having gotten over the shock of seeing the dead animal, he composed himself and carried on down the winding low-ceilinged dark tunnel, trembling with the cold, trying to hold back the tears that were forming in his eyes. He was also exhausted, and he had lost track of time, not knowing how long he'd been down there.

A few minutes later, he heard a loud rumbling sound in the distance, which made him catch his breath. He paused to try and work out where the noise was coming from. All of a sudden, dust and small flakes of dirt fell from the roof, and the walls began to vibrate. Not knowing what to expect, he quickly scaled up into a small opening in the wall. He shuffled his feet around the cramped space, firmly gripping the crumbling brickwork with one hand, while holding on tightly to the glass jar with the candle with the other. He kept perfectly still, bracing himself against the wall. *There it was again*, he thought, the rumbling sound growing louder and louder. The shaking of the walls made him think he was witnessing an underground earthquake. To his astonishment, in the inky darkness he could make out a four-foot high mountain of brown, filthy raging water rounding the final bend of the darkened tunnel. And to his horror, he realized that the level of that rushing, freezing water was the exact height of the small ledge he was precariously perched on.

The water was crashing against the walls, spewing up fountains of black spray high up into the air. His mouth fell open, his eyes bulging from their sockets. He shook his head, trying hard to focus on what he was doing as he desperately clung on to the narrow shelf.

The surging water was suddenly upon him, traveling at the speed of a train . . .

Unbeknownst to Thomas, the gallons of roaring murky water hurtling past him at a rate of knots had originated from the steep snowy hills directly behind the hall. So intense was its power, it had uprooted dozens of trees and torn out bushes from the snow-covered ground in its path, resulting in untold broken branches and vegetation, along with anything else in its wake, to end up charging down through the warren of tunnels beneath the hall.

Squinting and peering into the cloudy spray of water, he spotted a huge log twisting and bobbing around in the surging water heading his way, and knowing within a matter of seconds it would hopefully skip past him. He wedged his feet further into a hollow of the wall; his knees were pressed up against his chest. His feet were beginning to cramp from the strain of holding on, so he wiggled his legs and pulled them in as far as they would go, before quickly turning his head away from the spray, hoping the log would safely pass him by. Clenching his teeth and scrambling for a firmer hold with his small trembling fingers, he pulled his knees closer to his chest. Once again his feet were beginning to cramp up from being bent for so long.

He kept completely still on the ledge, aware that if the log knocked him off his perch, he would end up ducking and spluttering in the cold filthy water, which was the last thing he wanted. Plus, the added worry of not being able to swim made him feel more terrified.

Seconds later, feeling slightly bolder, he slowly shifted his body around to check whether the log had passed. It hadn't; it was still bobbing about in the swirling water a few inches away from him. In a blink of an eye, one of the twisted branches on the log hooked itself to the hem of his trouser leg, the momentum dragging him away from the safety of the ledge. Realizing what was going to happen, he quickly placed his other leg up against the wall before flattening himself against the opposite side, praying he would be able to hold on long enough while he struggled to unhook the branch from his jeans.

Due to the tremendous power of the water, he was finding it difficult to keep his balance. Once again, he dug his small groping fingers into the wet crumbling brickwork.

He was now becoming fearful and in some distress, as

his fingers were losing their grip, the log was beginning to drag him away from his ledge, and his other foot was gradually slipping away from its foothold, speeding up the inevitable.

The frustration and anger rising up in him caused his eyes to widen in sheer fright. It was the awful thought of not seeing his brothers and parents again that gave him the incentive to attack the log with brute force. Holding back the tears, bracing himself with what little strength he had left, he kicked out hard with his snagged leg. To his relief, he felt the grip that had him slip away. Pulling his dangling leg up to his chest, he began to wipe away the dirty water from the hem of his trousers, noticing that his fingertips were grazed and bloodied from all his frantic efforts. Thomas sat there, trying to compose himself after his awful ordeal, shaking with the thought of what could have happened. His wet hair clung in matted streaks to his forehead, and tears slowly crawled down his dirty cheeks. The sensation of being alive made him scream for joy. "Yippee!" he shouted at the top of his lungs, echoing down the dark tunnels.

Minutes later, the water had subsided, leaving him somewhat relieved. He repositioned his legs and rubbed them some more, trying to help ease the cramps that had set in. He then scrambled around in his coat pocket for a tissue, carefully wiping away the spray from his face and the dried-on blood stuck to the tips of his trembling fingers.

Satisfied there was no likelihood of any more surprises, he wiped his nose on the tissue and scanned the floor before pushing himself of the ledge, landing heavily on his feet with a bone-jarring jolt. He pitched forward onto his hands and knees, the glass jar slipping out of his hand into the slimy water.

"Oh, that's all I need right now!" he screamed, clenching his teeth to stop himself from crying out in pain.

Lifting himself out of the slime, he wiped his hands down the legs of his trousers, and using his wet forearm, mopped up a fresh crop of tears.

"Well, my jeans can't get any wetter and dirtier than they already are," he sobbed, feeling totally dejected.

Once calmed down, he successfully struck another match to one of the other candles he'd pulled out of his pocket. After checking himself over, satisfied that there weren't any sprains or broken bones, he placed his hands one at a time over the flame for some warmth as he made his way down the long dark passageway.

He was constantly grimacing at the stench of sewage and the sight of the rats that were running alongside him on a narrow brick ledge, eyeing him cautiously as they scuttled by. By now Thomas was getting used to them being around. He took several tentative steps forward, wading deeper into the flowing stream, the filthy water trickling into his sneakers. Up ahead he could only see an inky darkness, and his breath puffed past chattering teeth in clouds of vapor as he plunged further and further onward into the cold, smelly tunnels.

Thomas felt that the various passageways seemed to be going on forever. He couldn't see the end, and the heartache of no evidence of a draft coming from anywhere made him feel downhearted and abandoned by his brothers.

Moving along the tunnel, feeling its now all too familiar roughness and dampness with his cold trembling fingers, he felt as though he'd been on the run for hours. He stopped to catch his breath, the sound of his heart pounding in his ears. In the shadows around his feet, the tiny scuttling and scrabbling noises tested his nerves, his imagination running wild with thoughts of what was there. He began to shudder, and his hand trembled so much that he almost dropped the glass jar holding his precious candle.

Bending at the waist, staring down into the filthy water, he suddenly came up with an idea. *I know what I'll do. I'll follow the flow of the water. That way I may come across an opening to a river or some kind of an outlet,* he thought, now becoming excited with the prospect of escaping from the tunnels.

Having gotten his breath back, he set off in the direction of the current of the dirty water. As he rounded a corner, the light from the candle shone through the darkness to reveal a structure barring his path. Nearing the obstruction, the light revealed a tall fence-like gateway. He knew immediately by the thickness of the metal bars set into the wall that there was no way he would be able to break or bend them. And caught up in the thick wire grill was what seemed to be the log that had nearly swept him away. His first instinct was to walk away, but on second thought, he changed his mind and swaggered his way across, resembling a gunfighter. He kicked the log with such force that he ended up falling down, landing heavily, laughing out loud, and feeling a bit of an idiot. By now, he was feeling lonely and lost, yet he willed himself to stand up and carried on.

As he was considering what to do next, he sensed a breeze coming from above, chilling the sweat on the back of his neck and causing the candle to flutter. Peering up into the shadows, he spotted a faint light seeping out from what looked like a metal grate at the top of a long narrow dark shaft. He also spied a set of rusty well-worn ladders rising up from the floor and running up the side of the brick wall, reaching up into the darkness. He quickly came to the conclusion that the grate may be a manhole cover. He leaned back on the damp wall and burst into tears—but these tears were tears of joy.

Having controlled his emotions and breathing, he carefully gripped the glass jar safely with his small wet fingers before pulling himself up onto the first rung of the rickety rusty ladder.

The vibration of his ascent caused dirt and dust

from the crumbling brickwork to tumble down into his hair. He had to pause several times to wipe away the dust from his eyes and spit out a mouthful of dirt. He constantly checked to make sure the ladder wasn't going to come away from its foundations, knowing that if it did, heaven forbid, he would end up in a heap, injured and sprawled out at the bottom of the shaft. He moved upward, one slow, nervous step at a time, making sure he didn't slip and fall. To make matters worse, the movement and vibration of the ladder's supports had disturbed an army of sleepy cockroaches, the size of well-fed baby mice, to end up falling down from their hiding place into Thomas's hair. Some of them even found their way down the neck of his jacket.

"Ugh!" he cried out, desperately trying to brush away as many of them as he could without falling off the ladder.

Finally, he'd made it safely to the top of the ladder. Placing both feet at the ends of the rung of the ladder, and hooking his arm around the uppermost rung for support, he began to push the manhole cover upward. It was securely wedged in by the weeds and roots, which had become lodged around the edge of the lip over the years. He rested awhile, contemplating what his next move would be, reminding himself that he had to keep his cool, especially after what he'd just gone through. Composed and rested, he began to grab hold and pull away as many of the roots that were hanging down from the inside of the lip of the manhole cover. It took him fifteen sweaty and tiring minutes, extracting as many roots and weeds as he could, before resting again. Sweat was dripping down into his eyes, which made it difficult for him to see what he was doing.

Feeling more confident, he braced his feet once more on the rungs, and with one strong push, managed to dislodge and move the manhole cover a few inches before he stopped once again to take a rest. Having gotten his breath back, he tried once more, and with one massive effort, he eased the black dirty cover a few inches to one side.

Climbing up the last two rungs of the ladder, he poked his head up to check out the lay of the land, slyly peering over the edge into the cold and dark, the constant snowfall soaking his hair and clothes.

"I must look like a bedraggled old scarecrow," he giggled to himself as he began to clamber out of the hole.

He spent a few minutes ruffling his hair, hoping to dislodge any nasty creepy-crawlies that may still be lurking about in there, the relentless snowfall stinging his eyes.

After struggling to wrestle the manhole cover back into position, he decided to sit down and rest awhile on the packed snow to work out what was the best course of action. *Do I try and go back into the hall and hopefully free Jordan and James?* he thought. *Or do I go home and tell Mum and Dad what's happened to us all?*

After weighing up his options, he chose to go back home and tell his Mum and Dad, hoping they would be able to sort out the mess they were in like normal parents tended to do. But the way he was feeling right now, he wasn't all that confident.

Lifting himself up off the damp packed snow, brushing the melted snow from his hair and clothes, he cautiously headed toward a line of bushes, keeping as close as possible for some means of cover. His face and fingers were cold as ice, and he felt relief and terror at the same time, recalling the last sixty harrowing minutes.

He picked up his pace with swift strides; legs pumping up and down like pistons, kicking up clouds of snow. Sweat was beading down his face, and the back of his shirt was sticking to his clammy skin.

The snow was coming down in gusty diagonal streaks—enormous flakes the size of a child's fist. *If only the snow would stop,* he thought, chewing on his bottom lip.

Thomas knew he had to put as much distance between himself and the hall as possible, as he didn't want any of the dirty children to know what he was up to and see where he was going.

## Chapter Nineteen

Managing to reach the safety of the long winding path unscathed, Thomas stopped to take one last glance back at the hall before plodding on toward the lodge, all the while being careful that he didn't slip and fall on the ice hidden deep beneath the thick blanket of snow. His whole body was beginning to shake with the cold, and the awful thought of not seeing his brothers again brought further tears to his already moist eyes. Then, peering through the snow-covered trees, it seemed as though the lodge had also been rebuilt!

"This I don't need . . . it's giving me the heebie-jeebies' he cried. "Come on, you softy, I'm sure Mum and Dad will know what to do." His face glazed over with shock.

He paused a while longer to compose himself before trudging through the thick carpet of snow that had fallen while he had been trapped inside the hall, noticing that it had covered most of their footprints from the night before. With his head bent down, he strenuously made his way down the road, and hopefully, the safe sanctuary of his home, and more importantly, his parents.

Thomas was finding it difficult at first, stumbling through the thick snow. He could see virtually nothing, just the next few feet in front of him, his feet disappearing through new snow down to the older, compacted ice-hard layer below.

"Won't this snow ever stop?" gasped Thomas, mopping his wet brow with the back of his hand. His first instinct was to start running again, but because he was so exhausted and soaking wet, he stopped to lean against a lamppost, giving his aching muscles a moment to recover. Clouds of his hot breath puffed into the crisp winter air in front of him, and the weightless snowflakes danced randomly up and down, left and right.

Rested, he pushed himself into the onslaught of the relentless snow. Dead branches snapped left and right under his sneakers as he made his way as fast as he could.

Minutes later, he arrived at their back garden, wiping the snow from his face over and over again with his cold hands.

"Will Mum and Dad believe me?" he wheezed, winded by the exertion. *It does sound a bit far-fetched when you think about it, or am I dreaming?* he thought. "No," he said to himself after patting his frozen cheeks with the palm of his gloved hands. "Here goes," he muttered to himself, heading up the small path to the back door.

Making the short journey, he surprisingly spotted a child's pram along with an old dirty doll propped up inside. The pram was positioned where the tent should have been. *That's odd,* he thought, *I can't imagine Mum and Dad taking the tent down and not being out there searching for us with the police. And I don't recall anyone with a pram around here.*

He was just about to reach out to grab ahold of the handle to the back door when a young girl came dashing out of the house, shouting back over her shoulder to whoever was inside.

"I'm leaving this family; nobody loves me anymore!" It was then that she stopped mid-stride on the bottom step, spotting Thomas crouching down by the side of the back door, his head stuck between his knees, his body shivering.

"What the heck? Who are you, and what are you doing skulking out here?" snapped the girl, peering down at Thomas. "Do you know what time it is? You should be fast asleep in bed, not hanging around in other people's backyards," she continued, kneeling down beside him.

"What do you mean, 'Who are you?'" I could say the same thing to you; this is my back garden. I live here with my Mum and Dad and my two older brothers," snapped Thomas, suddenly becoming bold.

"Well, my name's Chelsea Scott, and I live here with *my* Mum and Dad and my irritating little sister, so get out of my garden—NOW!" she screamed, lifting herself up to her normal height, towering over Thomas.

"Who are you talking to, Chelsea?" asked the female voice coming from the inside of the house.

"No one important, Mum, just some little, wet, bedraggled street urchin I've found lurking in the back garden. I'll send him on his way; don't you worry yourself," she answered, gesturing with her hand for Thomas to move away from the house. As he was passing by the open doorway into the kitchen, Thomas peered inside, only to notice to his horror, a brightly colored calendar pinned to the wall with February 1988 blazoned in large bold type at the top of the page.

It was at this heart-stopping moment he knew that his Mum and Dad weren't in the house, and his two brothers may be trapped in the hall forever. Floods of tears suddenly came streaming down his cheeks, and he collapsed on the floor, crying out for his Mum and Dad.

"Hey, I didn't mean to scare you," said the girl in a warm, friendly manner, realizing she must have upset him.

"It's not you who's frightened me; it's just that my two older brothers are being held captive in Thorngarth Hall, and I need to get back there—quickly," hissed Thomas, sending a plume of condensation out before him.

"Thorngarth Hall's been abandoned for years; you must be mistaken. Come on, I'll take you home. It's getting late; your parents must be beside themselves with worry," she said, leading him away from the side of the house.

"This *is* my house, but a long time from now," replied Thomas, slyly edging away from the girl's grasp. A heavy feeling of dread rose up from the pit of his stomach.

"What's wrong with you, have you lost your marbles?" laughed the young girl, shaking her head in confusion.

"No, I haven't; I've lost my brothers and my Mum and Dad," cried Thomas, trying hard to release the girl's grip from his coat sleeve.

"Do you suffer from sleepwalking or are you on some kind of medication? You don't seem to be on the same planet as I am," said the girl, a look of shock on her face.

Thomas didn't bother answering, but quickly sprinted away, heading back to the hall, hopefully to be reunited with his brothers.

"Nutter," the girl called out to the fleeing form of Thomas as he was making his hasty retreat down the garden path.

"I hope Jordan and James are safe," murmured Thomas to himself, walking as fast as his little legs would go.

## Chapter Twenty

Once he'd accepted Jordan's pathetic apology about him knowing all along about the missing children, James lifted himself off the bed and took out a pocketknife from the back pocket of his jeans. It had a magnifying glass, a file, a little knife, scissors, and the attachment he was looking for: a screwdriver.

"Gotcha!" he called out in delight.

"What are you going to do with that James, dig your way out of here?" sniggered Jordan, pointing over at the knife.

"No, I'm not, poo head. If you'd been as observant as I was when we entered the room, you may have noticed the hinges on the door have been fixed to the inside of the door frame. So with a little bit of effort, I may be able to take out the screws, and then we can get out of this dump," smiled James, making his way across the dusty floor to the attic door.

Standing on his tiptoes, stretching up to reach the screws, James began to carefully peel away the dried on paint and rust, which had built up on them over the years. After an exerted and tricky effort, he eventually managed to ease all the screws away from the hinges, leaving the door to wobble in its frame.

"Please be careful," whispered James, while the rest of them were painstakingly unscrewing the last few turns with their small trembling fingers.

Jordan glanced across at James and gave him the thumbs-up sign. James acknowledged him with a friendly smile.

Once all the screws had been taken out, they lifted and dragged the door to one side, resting it against the bedroom wall carefully, as they didn't want anyone downstairs to hear what they were getting up to.

Satisfied that no one was likely to come up and investigate the noise they'd made, Amy and Adam dashed back to their beds to collect some additional clothing before hastily returning to join the rest of them, as they didn't want to be left behind. Scanning the inky stairway, the little group of adventurers cautiously and nervously advanced down the long, dark, winding corridor, hopefully to freedom. Jordan and Billy led the way, closely followed by the other three; all were praying they would find a safe passage out of the hall.

Minutes later, after blindly wandering around the numerous undecorated and rundown floors at the top of the hall, they surprisingly ended up back at the entrance to the attic. They all stared at one another, looking totally confused and utterly dejected.

"Jordan, what's happened? I thought you said you

knew the way out of this place," said James, sneaking a quick look into the attic, ensuring no one was inside, especially Thomas.

"Be quiet, James. I can see what's happened; I'm not that thick. I need to think this through," snapped Jordan, glancing back over his shoulder to where they'd come from.

'That's it; I can remember now," cried Jordan, instructing them with a wave of his hand to move closer so they could hear what he had to say. "When we were being herded up here to the attic, I noticed dozens of passageways leading off in all directions, and that's the reason why we've ended up back here . . . we're lost," proclaimed Jordan, with a defeatist shrug of his shoulders, walking away from the group.

"So that's it then Jordan? We're lost. Is that all you have to say? Come on, guys, we need to find a way of getting out of this place, and I think I may have just the answer," announced James, pulling out two sticks of white chalk from his coat pocket.

"Squirrel to the rescue once again," said Jordan, looking across at James with pride.

"James, how are two pieces of chalk going to get us out of here?" asked Amy, with a look of confusion across her face.

After handing over one of the pieces of chalk to Jordan, James came across to explain his cunning plan to Amy.

"I realize two sticks of chalk won't be as effective as two sticks of dynamite, but they may aid us in finding a way out of this mess we're in. What we're going to do is draw a marker on the walls as we head down the corridors and landings, and when we come across a chalk mark, we will know not to go that way again, and we'll head off in another direction. Hopefully we will end up downstairs, to safety." James didn't wait for a reply, but wrapped his arm around her, affectionately squeezing her, before moving back over to Jordan.

Amy, on the other hand, gazed across into James's eyes, whispering, "Thank you, James. Sorry—Squirrel." Tears were now running down her cheeks, which she wiped away with the tips of her fingers.

Apart from the sound of their feet on the bare wooden floor, the rest of the hall was silent as a grave. Then, somewhere down the dark corridor, a ghostly whispering sound could be heard. Jordan quickly indicated with his hand for them to stop.

"What is it?" mouthed Billy, his arms blossoming with goose bumps.

"I've no idea; just stay where you are and keep your voices down. Hopefully, whatever it is will go away," whispered Jordan to the terrified group.

Jordan narrowed his eyes and stared into the darkness, trying to work out where the noise was coming from.

"There it is again, Jordan," muttered James, clamping his hand over his mouth to stop himself from screaming out in fright.

For the next few minutes, no one dared move or say a word, as they were terrified of what could be creeping around down the corridor.

Jordan eventually found the nerve to venture down to investigate the noise, instructing the rest to stay well hidden in the shadows of the corridor.

Hugging the wall, making sure he wasn't going to trip and fall on the loose, worn carpet, Jordan noticed up ahead a door that was slightly ajar, quickly figuring out that the noise must be coming from in there. Cunningly, he dropped down on all fours, scrambling on his hands and knees across the rough carpet. Carefully, he peered underneath the crack at the bottom of the door, hoping to see if there was anyone lurking about inside. Thankfully, he couldn't see anyone. *I'll count to twenty,* he thought, *and if it's still silent when I've finished counting—if it is completely, utterly quiet—then . . . well, maybe I'll check the room out.*

When he'd finished counting to twenty, he slowly crawled toward the edge of the door, peeking around the side, making sure there was no one hiding inside the room.

"Nothing; thank goodness for that," he said under his breath, wiping the sweat from his forehead.

The only noise he could hear now was the flapping sound of a curtain next to an open window at the back of the room. He took a few tentative steps inside, only to reveal a spacious room with high windows containing two large high-backed chairs positioned in front of a blazing fire, a tall wooden wardrobe, and a writing desk. The walls were lined with the heads of stuffed animals with glazed eyes gazing down out of wooden mounts.

He stood for a few seconds just inside the doorway, blinking as his eyes adjusted to the dim light. It was silent except for the occasional gust of wind coursing through the open window. Meanwhile, the other four had become impatient, so they'd decided to make their way down the corridor.

While Jordan was taking one final look around the gloomy room, he heard the sounds of movement coming from the corridor. To his relief, James appeared in the doorway, quickly followed by Billy, and making up the band of warriors, Amy and Adam.

As they were snooping around the room, James came upon the writing desk, and lying on the top was an old brown-stained newspaper.

The heading on the front page made James's head swim, his legs began to shake, and his heart to pound like a road drill in his chest.

## Evening Chronicle
## February 29th, 1980

**The children of Lord and Lady Popple-Brownlow mysteriously disappear in the area bordering Thorngarth Hall**

> Fears are growing for the safety of Lord and Lady Popple-Brownlow's two young children, who have been missing since early yesterday afternoon.
> They were last seen by their parents when the children decided to go for a leisurely stroll shortly after lunch.
> So far the police are refusing to make any connection between this and the unsolved disappearance of the children and their guardians from Thorngarth Hall in 1968. "We see no reason to link this case with any other at this stage," said Inspector Ashby, heading the inquiry. "It would be fair to say, however, that we keep an open mind on these matters."

James's hands began to shake and he was unable to speak, his stomach knotting up. He let out a pent up breath and turned to face Jordan.

By this time, Jordan was trying to climb up the stone wall to see how far the drop was from the open window. Unfortunately, when he'd reached the grimy window, he noticed that there were iron bars set into the concrete on the outside. Glumly, he jumped down and made his way over toward James, who was still in a state of shock. As Jordan approached him, he couldn't help but notice the frozen expression on James's face.

"What's the matter with you, James? You look as though you've seen a ghost," he said sarcastically.

James didn't say a word, but handed over the newspaper to Jordan, pointing a shaky finger at the headlines on the front page.

After reading the first few lines of the article, Jordan held his fingers up to his lips to stop James from saying anything to the other three, as he didn't want to upset them.

"Come on; let's get out of here while we can," whispered Jordan, carefully placing the newspaper back on the desk.

"Yes, move your butts, all of you," ordered Billy, ushering them over to the door.

Suddenly, there was a noise, which made them all stop what they were doing. It was the sound of a chair being scraped across a wooden floor in the next room. Several seconds passed with all five straining to detect the slightest movement. They stood in silence until Jordan brought them out of their trance.

"Hide! I think someone's in the next room, and I've got an awful feeling they're coming out," hissed Jordan, his eyes transfixed with horror.

None of them needed to be told twice, so they began to search the room for somewhere to hide. They were finding it difficult at first, as they all headed toward the large wooden wardrobe. Realizing there was only enough space for three of them to hide inside, James and Jordan quickly made their way over to the two high-backed chairs positioned next to the open fire. Thick woolen shawls had been draped over the backs, and as luck would have it, they were so long that they reached all the way to the dusty floor. After crawling on their hands and knees and hiding behind the two chairs, they wrapped the shawls around their heads and shoulders.

Jordan was shaking with fear, the blood draining from his face as the door handle from the next room began to rattle and turn, combined with the sounds of shuffling feet outside in the corridor. Jordan looked across to where James was concealed. Their eyes met; Jordan raised a finger to his lips, gesturing to James to be still and be very, very quiet.

## Chapter Twenty-One

"Mind your elbows, young man, and please give me some room to move," snapped Amy as she was attempting to ease her way further toward the back of the smelly wardrobe.

"Look, if you don't stop moaning, I'll open the wardrobe door and throw you out on your posh backside," giggled Billy, trying his best not to sneeze from all the hairs floating around from the fur coats hanging up in the cramped wardrobe.

"Quiet, both of you, I can hear voices and the sound of running feet coming from the corridor," muttered Adam, biting his lip and rubbing his nose to stop himself from sneezing.

"Sir, sir, miss, I've just been upstairs to check on the children we locked up the attic, and they've escaped. They've somehow cleverly managed to take the door of its hinges, and they must be hiding somewhere in the hall," barked Scally, taking a step back from the two angry looking adults.

"Scally, get down to the cellar and bring that little brat back up here; at least we'll have one of them. I can't imagine the others leaving the hall without him. Also, there's still time to find the other five. Split into four groups and search all of the rooms. Don't all of you go in the same direction; spread yourselves out. If you do happen to find them, get word back to me as soon as you can. Then we can all grab a few hours sleep before sun-up."

The old man and woman began to shuffle the dirty children around to form four groups.

"And who's left this door open? How many times do I have to remind you about keeping all the doors shut in the hall at this time of the year," bellowed the old man, sneering at the terrified children gathered around him. He quickly stepped inside; his smoldering eyes examining the room. Satisfied that the room was deserted, he slammed the door shut with an almighty crash, causing the walls to vibrate, and then securely locked it. With a sweeping hand gesture, he indicated for the children to move away and start searching the hall.

While the old man was ranting and raving at the children outside in the corridor, James and Jordan stared at one another, eyes like Frisbees, aware that there was no chance of them getting out of room now that it had been locked.

Confident that there was no likelihood of anyone coming in to search the room, James pulled the shawl away from his shoulders and lifted himself up from the floor, brushing away the dirt from the knees of his jeans.

"You can come out now," whispered James, easing open the door of the wardrobe a crack, making sure that the hinges didn't squeak in the process.

Billy was the first one out, covering his eyes, trying to adjust them from the darkness he'd been in for the past few minutes. Adam and Amy soon followed, a look of fear spread across their faces.

"Am I correct in thinking that they have locked the door, James?" asked a terrified Amy, her facial muscles twitching nervously.

James didn't have the heart to tell her the bad news, so he began to pace the room, trying to come up with a way of getting them out of this mess.

Approaching the locked door, he stopped to kneel down and peer through the keyhole. Then, easing himself up off the floor, he headed across to the table where the newspaper had been left and picked it up before tucking it under his arm.

"I think I may have a way of getting us out of here," he happily informed the group, indicating with his hand for them to move a little closer so he wouldn't have to raise his voice.

Certain he had their undivided attention; James began to explain his idea to them.

"We're fortunate; the stupid old man has left the key in the lock. So I'm hoping, with the aid of my sturdy knife, I may be able to maneuver the key in the keyhole so that it will fall onto the floor, and that's when this newspaper will come in handy. We do have a slight problem, though. If anyone is hanging about outside in the corridor, they'll soon know we're in here and then we'll be caught. But at the moment, I can't come up with anymore ideas. Unless any of you have a better one?" he asked, waiting for an answer, his heart fluttering in his chest.

"James, what are you going to do with the newspaper?" asked a puzzled looking Amy, her eyes shooting up in surprise.

"I was going to ask that question . . . *well*, what are you going to do with it?" mocked Billy.

"Billy, if you had spent more time at school using your brain instead of your fists, you may have been the one to have worked out a way of getting us out of here," James replied gruffly, pulling a face at Billy.

Billy wasn't used to having someone stick up for themselves, and it took him a while to respond to James's remark.

"I've a good mind to punch you on the nose, but I will let you off this time, Waldron. So, come on then, what are you going to do with the newspaper?" he asked embarrassingly, digging his nails into the palms of his hands.

"I'm going to slide a few inches of it underneath the door, and when the key drops out onto the floor, hopefully it will fall onto the newspaper. Then we will carefully slide the paper back into the room, and presto!

We will have the key." James stood there waiting for applause, but all he got was a friendly handshake and a pat on the back from Billy, which James accepted with a nod and a friendly smile.

James opened the newspaper and separated a few of the pages, as he didn't want it to be too thick that it wouldn't slide under the door. He also turned the front page face down so that Amy and Adam didn't see the bold headlines.

Once ready, they made their way toward the door, all the while listening out for any movement coming from outside in the corridor.

James slowly crouched down onto his knees and placed his right eye against the keyhole, expecting to see signs of movement outside in the dimly lit corridor.

"It seems to be quiet out there at the moment, so here goes. Keep your fingers crossed, all of you," he suggested as he laid the paper out onto the dusty floor.

Very, very carefully, he slowly slid the newspaper under the foot of the door a few inches at a time; holding his breath, sweat beading on his brow. Confident there was no one lurking in the corridor, James quickly pulled out his knife from the back pocket of his jeans and selected the screwdriver attachment.

Before he started to jiggle the key about, James wiped away the sweat from the palms of his hands down the sleeves of his jacket. Once composed, he began to fiddle with the key. He was having to do it all by touch, plus he had no way of being able to see what he was doing, as there was very little light, and also the opening of the keyhole was small. Five heart stopping minutes had passed and James was still at it.

"James, do you want to take a rest and let me have a try?" asked Jordan, glancing over James's shoulder.

"I . . . think . . . it's . . . coming . . . out . . . now . . ."

THUD!

Lifting himself up from the floor, James stretched his back and rubbed the cramps from his legs, leaving Jordan and Billy to pull the newspaper, and more importantly the key, safely back into the room.

"You are a genius, James," cooed Amy, wrapping her arms around him, planting a kiss on both cheeks. James wasn't used to having strange girls hugging and kissing him, but in this case he made an exception, and enjoyed it.

"Come on, we need to get out of this room as quickly as possible. I can well imagine the grubby kids coming back here to search this room at some stage when they can't find us," urged Jordan, sweat trickling down from under his armpits.

Satisfied they were all ready to go, James turned the key in the lock and eased the door open, checking up and down the corridor to ensure that the coast was clear.

"Keep together and listen out for any movement at all. We are very close to getting out of here, and we can't afford to get caught now, especially after all we've been through tonight," stated Jordan, shutting the door and locking it. He then bent down and skimmed the key under the door into the room.

Slowly panning the dreary scene in front of him, Jordan instructed the group to make their way down the gloomy corridor. There seemed to be dozens of doorways leading into different rooms, and none of them wanted to know what was skulking around inside them. They half-walked, half-trotted down a cramped and sloping corridor, the faint moonlight coming through windows high up near the vaulted ceiling was casting an eerie glow across the wooden floor. The floorboards creaked under their feet, and there was nothing to absorb the noise, just bare walls and bare floors.

At one panic-stricken stage, they spotted mysterious shadowy outlines approaching them from the landing, and they heard hushed voices and hysterical mutterings. Fortunately, the shadows and voices moved in the opposite direction from the small band of worried children.

Many minutes later, after going up and down and around and around in circles, they eventually reached the bottom of the staircase that led to the first floor landing. James was patted on the back by the rest of the team, acknowledging that his quick thinking may have got them to safety. James shrugged his shoulders and waved his hand in the air, brushing away their praise, and also feeling proud of himself.

"Sssh, I think I can hear some movement downstairs in the hall," said Jordan, his fingers pressed up against his lips.

He turned to face the group, whispering, "Stay here while I go downstairs and investigate, okay?"

They all nodded their agreement and moved a safe distance back into the shadows of the landing, carefully listening out for any movement from within the upstairs rooms, as it had become deathly quiet.

Placing his left hand on the faded wallpaper for support, Jordan stealthily crept down the stairs, making sure his feet were positioned as close to the edge of the wooden stairs as possible, as he didn't want them to creak under his weight, and praying that there wasn't anything too scary down there waiting for him . . .

Crouching down near the foot of the stairs, he stole a glance through the gap in the banister and spied three large black Doberman dogs wandering aimlessly around the hall. They were hunched down, their noses pressed down to the dusty floor; they were sweeping from left to right like metal detectors, all searching for a scent to follow. No doubt they'd been left there to stop anyone from escaping through the front door, Jordan presumed.

Cautiously and quietly, he turned around and made his way stealthily back up the stairs. On reaching the safety of the landing, he tiptoed his way toward the frightened looking children who had been patiently waiting for him. He indicated for them to close ranks so they could hear what he had to say.

"What is it, Jordan? You don't look too happy," said a worried James, even before Jordan could open his mouth.

"There's three, fierce looking black dogs roaming around at the bottom of the stairs and along the corridor. They're blocking our path to the front door," shrugged Jordan, shaking his head in surrender.

"Don't worry about that; just you wait here and don't move. I know what to do," ordered James, moving down the corridor, and at the same time ferreting around in his coat pockets for any more leftover biscuits.

"James, you can't go down there; those dogs will attack you. Come back . . ." Jordan called out softly. James had already disappeared.

James stood rooted at the top of the stairs, not daring to move. He held his breath and peeked around the corner of the wooden banister to check out what was happening below. Delighted that there was no signs of human life, he carried on down the stairs. Two steps from the bottom, the stair creaked; he stopped short, his heart pounding. Then a branch slapped against a window above him and James's jaw clenched. "It's just the wind," he muttered to himself.

Once the dogs had spotted him, they began to gracefully glide over to him, white foam slowly dribbling out from the sides of their powerful jaws onto the wooden floor. Acting and feeling bold, James offered the biscuits to the three dogs, carefully dropping them onto the dusty wooden floor and well away from their escape route to the front door. While he was doing all of this, he carefully lifted up his jumper and unbuttoned his shirt before slipping a small biscuit crumb by the side of the sleeping mouse, which was nestled in the folds of his shirt. "Here you are, something you can nibble on when you wake up, instead of scratching me," he whispered, carefully buttoning up his shirt.

"Jordan, Jordan, can you hear me? Slowly and very, very carefully make your way down the stairs. The dogs are busy eating my biscuits. Can you hear me Jordan, Jordan?" called out James as loud as he dared, both hands cupped around his mouth.

Within seconds of him beckoning them down, the worried looking face of Jordan appeared from around the top of the banister, followed by the other three. Satisfied that the dogs didn't seem to be any kind of threat—for the time being at least—Jordan instructed them to hold hands and slowly make their way down the stairs.

As Jordan was passing James, he bent down and whispered in his ear, smiling in admiration. "Well done, Squirrel; I can always rely on you when the going gets tough."

James looked up to see Jordan's smiling face, moisture glistening in both their eyes. "No prob, big brother. I'm always here to help," replied James, wiping the remains of the biscuits from his sticky hands onto the dusty floor.

It was the sudden unexpected opening of a number of upstairs bedroom doors, combined with the echo of dozens of stamping feet on the landing that made the five children freeze just feet away from the front door.

"Run, and follow me!" shouted Jordan, quickly grabbing ahold of James by the hand, as he didn't want to lose him again.

They all turned and fled, slipping on the wet floor in the process. Jordan was hoping the door hadn't been locked while they'd been trapped inside, and if not, praying the gap he'd left was wide enough for him to get his hand around. Knowing that he had only a few seconds before the manic looking dirty children would reach them, he began to wonder what would become of them if they were caught. *Doesn't bear thinking about,* he thought, knowing he had to get himself, his brothers, plus the other three out of the hall before sunrise, and more importantly, they had to find Thomas, and soon.

Luckily, the door was as they'd left it.

"Come on, guys, they'll be onto us soon," cried Billy, glancing back over his shoulder at the manic pack of children stampeding down the stairs. He noticed some of them were taking two to three steps at a time in their haste to reach the fleeing prisoners, which made him start to panic.

"Come on, come on, move it," screamed Billy, watching the children with wild-eyed terror.

With an exerted effort from Jordan, the door eventually eased open, and they made their hasty escape into the cold, wintry night.

"You won't get very far out there," called out the old man as he was making his way down the steep winding staircase. "None of you know the secret of getting back to the year you all came from . . . you're all trapped!" His hysterical laughter was fading behind them as they headed toward a cluster of snow-covered bushes.

Keeping hold of James's trembling hand, and with a quick glance at the others, Jordan ordered them to follow him through the thick carpet of snow, well away from the hall.

"There's a load of tall hedges over there," he informed them. "We'll go over in that direction. Hopefully there'll be enough foliage for us to disappear into, and then we'll just have to come up with a plan as quickly as possible so we can all go home. But that's only after we get Thomas out of this horrible place," he added, his breath pluming before him in the cold early morning air.

"Jordan, what did the old man mean when he said we don't have the secret to get back home? I didn't like the sound of that," inquired James, looking puzzled, trying very hard to get his breath and composure back.

It was at this point Adam stepped closer to them all,

shaking his head, fear evident on his cold face.

"Thanks guys for getting us out of the attic, but unfortunately your brother is right, we don't have the secret of getting out of this place. We managed to escape once before, but when we reached the lodge and the main road, everything was old. We can only get out once we know the secret, if not, we're all going to be in here for a very long time." Adam inched his way toward his sister, sensing she was becoming upset.

"While you've both been stuck in here, has the old man or woman given you any idea to what the secret may be?" Jordan asked, examining their terrified faces, hoping for some kind of clue.

"Just the once, but I can't remember everything they said; it's been so long," answered Adam, looking away from the group, feeling as though he had let them all down.

"Just let me stop and think for a while, will you? I may be able to remember," remarked Amy, trying hard to recall all the words.

"Let's not worry too much about that at the moment, but keep thinking about it anyway, won't you?" commented James, not really believing either of them. "What we need to do is hide somewhere and try to work out how to get out of here," remarked James, realizing it most certainly would have been a much better idea if he had stayed in the tent. Yet, knowing that he had his big brother with him made him feel slightly less frightened, but he also knew they had to find Thomas—and quickly.

Fortunately for them, it had stopped snowing, leaving the gusting wind to blow away the clouds, giving them enough light from the glow of the moon to see where they were walking.

After a few nervous minutes, they managed to find their way into a large cluster of hedges, which reminded James of a maze he and Thomas had visited recently on a school trip.

"I think this is far enough, don't you?" asked Jordan, carefully surveying the area around for anything untoward.

"What time is it, Jordan?" asked James, the look of fear masked across his little face.

"Oh great, that's all we need! My watch is smashed," shouted Jordan, glancing down at his wrist. "I must have broken it as we were making our way out of the hall. Has anyone else got the time?" asked Jordan, scanning the worried faces circling him.

"What about your cell phone, Jordan?" cried James, jumping up and down on the spot, helping to keep himself warm.

"Good thinking, Batman . . . just hold on a minute. I'll ring Mum and Dad; they can come over and collect us all. Why didn't I think of that before?" proclaimed Jordan, now becoming excited, and also annoyed at himself for not using his cell phone in the first place.

"What's a cell phone?" inquired Adam, staring down at the odd looking contraption in Jordan's hand.

"Jeez, how long have you been stuck here?" asked Jordan, glancing down at the phone, waiting for a signal to appear on the illuminated screen.

"We've been trapped in here since 1980. Look, guys, we just want to go home; please find a way of helping us get out of this horrible place," pleaded Adam, tears beginning to stream down his face.

"I can't promise that we will get you out of this mess," stated Jordan, "but we are going to have a damn good try, and in the process we'll make it as difficult as possible for Scally and the Scallywags and the two ugly, revolting, dog poo-faced twins in there to catch us."

The tension in the group relaxed a little after Jordan's funny remark, making them giggle as they walked around, trying to keep warm.

"I can't get a signal on my phone!" exclaimed Jordan. "It's completely dead."

"How long have those things been around?" asked Amy, slipping the phone out of Jordan's hand to examine it, and holding it as though it may burn her numb fingers.

"They've been around for a while now; nearly everyone has one; some people have two. I've even heard that some have three of them, greedy so-and-so's," replied Jordan.

"Anyway, if you think my cell phone looks weird,

just wait until you see the other gadgets that are available. That's once we're out of this horrible nightmare," said Jordan, snapping his useless phone shut, and slipping it into his back pocket of his jeans.

"Never mind. Hey, we're not beaten yet," proclaimed James, thinking, *This can't be happening; it cannot be real.*

In all the excitement, James had completely forgotten about his furry little friend who was nestled in the folds of his shirt. He decided not to mention anything to Jordan or the rest of the group, just in case they asked him to let it loose, which he didn't want to do.

"I've just realized something!" proclaimed Jordan. "If those creepy kids decide to come out of the hall and search for us, they will soon be able to see where we're headed by following our footprints in the snow. Come on; start kicking the snow around. Try to disturb as much of it as possible; hopefully, that will confuse them."

It was a cold, cold night, yet sweat was forming on all of their brows from struggling around in the deep snow.

Satisfied that the snow in their immediate area was churned up sufficiently to cause anyone to wonder which direction the fleeing group had headed for, they cautiously moved away from the horrible, creepy building.

"Jordan, just hold on a moment. I thought I heard the sounds of breaking branches and moaning coming from those bushes over there . . . get ready, we may have to leg it," mumbled James, indicating the location of the noise with a quick jerk of his head.

They heard the crack of a branch; its brittle snap echoed deep within the bushes. Something or someone was moving around in the darkness.

"Can you see anything, James?" asked a nervous Jordan, his heart pounding away like a hammer inside his chest.

## Chapter Twenty-Two

"Jordan, James, am I happy to see you two!" wheezed Thomas as he fought his way out of the undergrowth on his hands and knees.

"Thomas!" cried James with joy. "What are you doing groveling around in there? And we'd thought we'd lost you for good," continued James, running over to help Thomas remove the snow from his hair and coat, then hugging him closely before giggling and swinging him around in the snow.

After regaining his balance, Thomas moved toward the welcoming open arms of Jordan, mopping the snow from his hands on a soggy tissue.

"It's too upsetting for me to tell you everything that's happened to me, but all I can say is that I finally managed to escape from the cellar by going through the dark, scary tunnels under the hall. Luckily, I found a box of matches and a few candles. They definitely came in handy, as it was pitch black down there in the tunnels. When I eventually found my way out, I decided to go back home, and guess what? Mum and Dad don't live there anymore! There was this creepy girl coming out of the back door, and she said she lived there, not us . . ." Thomas broke down in tears, reliving the harrowing encounter he had just gone through.

Jordan gently placed an arm around Thomas's shoulder. "It's good to see that you're safe and well and back with us both. Don't worry, Tom, and try not to get upset, we'll get out of this mess somehow, you just wait and see," mumbled Jordan weakly, choking back his own tears, grinning as best he could. Deep down, Jordan wasn't at all confident.

"While I was escaping from the tunnels . . ." Thomas stammered to a halt, staring in shock at the children who were cowering behind Jordan and James.

"Where did they come from? And isn't that Billy Three . . . there are three of you," Thomas gasped, blinking with surprise, realizing what he was about to say.

"We haven't got the time to explain the whole facts, but let's just say we don't want to be hanging around this place for too long, or else we're going to be stuck here for the next four years!" whispered Jordan to a frightened looking Thomas. He didn't dare mention how Adam and Amy came to be held captive in the hall; he just hoped and prayed that Thomas didn't question him about them.

"Come on, Jordan, let's head over to my house. You never know, Tom may have gone to the wrong one," remarked Billy, making his way down the snow-covered path.

"Hey, what do you mean by that? Do you think I'm stupid or something? I know where I live; I'm not that dumb," exclaimed Thomas, darting over to Billy and punching him on the arm. Billy responded by lunging at him, trying to punch Thomas back.

"Stop it, both of you! We're in enough trouble as it is without you two fighting each other," shouted Jordan, attempting to pull them apart.

"What do you suggest we do now, Jordan?" asked James, brushing the snow from his hair.

"I think the best thing for us to do is to go back to our house and see if Thomas was telling us the truth. He may have gone to the wrong address; you know what Thomas is like when he's tired," smiled Jordan, tilting his head to one side, waiting for some kind of sarcastic reply from Thomas.

"What was that you said, Jordan? I know where I live; I'm not that thick," shrugged Thomas from the insult that had been thrown at him.

"I didn't say you were thick, but you have had a nasty scare tonight. We all have, so you could have ended up at the wrong address. Come on, let's go and see," suggested Jordan, knowing he couldn't come up with anything better at the moment.

"All right, if only to show you all that I wasn't lying, and I'm not thick," mumbled Thomas under his breath.

"Jordan, look over there at the lodge; that seems to

have been restored as well," said Billy, as they were only a short distance from the main gate. "Or are my eyes deceiving me?"

"I don't like this one little bit," commented Thomas. "I noticed it earlier on when I passed it on my way home."

Mindful that Thomas was frightened, Jordan wrapped his arm around him, glancing down, saying to them all, "Keep calm everyone; once we get safely back home, Mum and Dad will know what to do. I'm pretty sure of it."

"I do hope so," said James, the look of uncertainty spread all over his face.

"I think it may be wise if you three stay back there at the lodge, while we go and check out our house," suggested Jordan. "I don't think it will look too good if someone spots us all, especially at this time in the morning. What do you say?"

They all agreed that was probably the best course of action. So, Billy, along with Adam and Amy, made their way into the lodge, collecting on the way the blankets that had been left strewn all over the floor by the brothers. The remnants of the fire was just about nearing its end, which didn't go down too well with Billy, as there were no more newspapers and twigs left over to relight it. Instead, they wrapped the blankets around their shoulders and stepped into the next room, making themselves as comfortable as possible on the restored couch, snuggling up to each other to keep warm.

As the three brothers marched down the road, they were shocked to see that there were no signs of life or any cars driving by. "Strange," whispered Jordan under his breath.

"Are you certain you went to the correct house, Thomas?" asked James. "You have had a bad fright tonight, you know?"

"Of course I am. What do you take me for, a complete fool? Don't answer that, James; I can read your mind," sniggered Thomas, rubbing his arms, trying to circulate the blood in his cold veins.

During the course of the next ten minutes, the brothers toiled through the thick banks of snow. Luckily for them, the cold wind had died down, which made the early morning air feel a touch warmer.

"Sssh, both of you, we're nearly close to home, and from where I'm standing, it doesn't look the same as it did last night when we left. I've got a nasty feeling Thomas may have been telling us the truth all along. Sorry, Thomas, for doubting you," apologized Jordan, which was quickly echoed by James.

"You don't have to apologize, guys, I just want to get things back to normal," muttered Thomas, blowing into his cupped hands.

Gingerly approaching the black metal gate that led to the house, they all stopped, suddenly realizing that their gate had been made of wood.

"Jordan . . . James, I think it would be best if we

made a run for it back to the lodge and met up with the others," said a nervous sounding Thomas, knowing what would be in store for them if the nasty girl came out and caught them.

# Chapter Twenty-Three

"I thought I told you to leave . . .?" called out the young girl, leaning out from one of the bedroom windows. "Shouldn't you three be tucked up fast asleep in bed, instead of sneaking around someone else's back garden?" she added. "Just stay where you are, and don't move a muscle; I'm coming down," she ordered, before closing the window.

They thought it wouldn't be a good idea if they ran out of the garden. They were in enough trouble as it was, and they didn't want to make it any worse for themselves. So they waited nervously in the cold to check out what the girl had to say.

It was Thomas who broke the cold, deathly silence.

"You didn't believe me, did you? Mum and Dad don't live here. We've somehow managed to go back in time," sobbed Thomas, as the back door flew open with the girl appearing, buttoning up her coat.

"Come on, you three, get inside the house this minute. I'm going to call the police; let them sort this mess out," she said, attempting to keep the back door open for them to enter, ensuring she was closely positioned behind the three of them, preventing them from escaping.

"Who do you think we are, hooligans? You don't even know us. Please let us go," pleaded James, tears forming in his eyes.

Once inside, the three brothers stopped to survey the room; instantly knowing by the outdated kitchen furniture and old-fashioned wallpaper that they were in the right house, but in the wrong year. And when Jordan spotted the 1988 calendar pinned to the wall, he was also aware that they were in some deep, serious, trouble . . .

Thomas began to cry for his Mum.

"Don't be such a cry baby. You should have thought about the consequences before I caught you wandering around outside. Especially after telling you off earlier on this morning; how many times do you need telling?" the young girl mocked, scowling over at the them. Yet at the back of her mind, she had a nagging feeling that things weren't at all as they seemed.

Moving nervously toward the girl, Jordan asked in a calm, pleading voice for her to sit down and listen to what he had to say, so he could at least give her the facts of what had happened to them all during the course of the past few hours.

Reluctantly, she agreed to his pleading, pulling up a chair to the kitchen table and slumping down. During his unbelievable narrative, Thomas and James interrupted the flow of the conversation, each of them adding their own frightening experiences.

After ten tense minutes, they came to the end of their story, leaving the girl to fidget in her chair, staring up at the ceiling, recalling hearing about the infamous hall from some of her schoolmates. At the time she thought they were pulling her chain. *Or were they?* she wondered, scanning the three young worried faces in front of her.

"I can't decide whether to believe you or not, but I can't imagine someone as young as you three making up such a fantastic story in the first place. Come on, let's head over to the hall; I want to check it out. Let me see for myself whether you've been lying to me or not," demanded the girl, easing herself out of the chair.

"Is Chelsea your real name?" inquired Thomas, as he was elbowing his way out of the back door. He didn't want to be in *this* house any longer than he had to.

"Yes. It's an awful name isn't it? It was Dad who thought of it. I can't see it catching on, can you?" she inquired, shocked that someone his age would ask her in the first place.

"You'd be surprised," answered Thomas, under his breath.

"What was that?" she asked, clicking her tongue in annoyance.

"Nothing, I'm just mumbling to myself... as usual," replied Thomas, smiling.

"Boys, ugh! I know a shortcut through the cemetery; hopefully we can reach the hall before sunrise; if not, you're going to be hanging around here a little bit longer than you expected, and to be honest, that's the last thing I want at the moment. No offense, boys."

"None taken." echoed the brothers, wishing their nightmare would soon come to an end.

# Chapter Twenty-Four

Walking as fast as their legs would carry them, the group of three terrified boys and one suspicious young girl headed toward the cemetery, hopefully without anything untoward happening to them on the way.

Ten exhausting minutes later, the cemetery suddenly rose up in front of them. Granite gravestones were dotted around the rolling hillside. There was row after row of grave markers, and tall, weather-beaten, ugly monuments visible in the grounds. Most of them seemed to be stained by decades of pigeon droppings as well as a thick layer of snow. There was evidence of tangled coarse dead weeds emerging from the snow, and cellophane wrapped flowers had been carefully laid on top of a number of newly dug graves. Fortunately for them, there came a break in the clouds, which left the bright moon to illuminate the graveyard and gave off a ghostly radiance around the grounds.

"The more I think about what you have told me tonight, the more I am convinced that you must be on some kind of medication. You only read about weird and frightening things in kid's horror books; they should never happen in real life," the girl commented as they carefully edged their way through the opening of the rusty gates to the graveyard. The four-foot snowdrifts was making it difficult for them to ease the gate open.

"Quiet, all of you, and don't move an inch. I'm sure I saw something dash behind that large stone angel over there by the wall," whimpered Thomas, glancing over toward the spot that was hidden in the shadow of a tall oak tree.

"Thomas, we haven't got time for silly games. We're in enough trouble as it is; we don't want any more scary surprises," snapped Jordan, carefully weaving his way around the gravestones.

"I don't think Thomas is lying. Look, I can see a number of eerie shadows scuttling just over by those gravestones," murmured James, wide eyed and shaking with fear.

Jordan gingerly placed his hands on top of Thomas and James's shoulders, gently pushing them down to the ground so the owners of those shadows may not be aware of their presence at the moment.

All four stealthily walked crab-like toward the shadows, with Jordan collecting a thick branch on the way.

As they inched their way closer to the stone wall, a shadowy figure jumped out from behind an eight-foot marble monument over to their left, causing all four to scream out in fright.

"Boo!" a voice boomed out from the shadows.

It was Billy what's-his-name!

"You stupid, stupid idiot!" screamed Jordan, standing rigid with terror. "You frightened the life out of us then! What are you doing hiding in here? I thought you were going to wait for us back at the lodge," barked Jordan, trying to control his anger, his hands balled into tight fists.

"I thought it would be best to move out of the lodge, because the two old cronies came out of the hall and they seemed to be heading in our direction. So we moved well away from there, and when we came upon this place, we thought it would be best to wait in here for you for a while before we returned to the lodge. Anyway, who's the girl? Your new girlfriend, Jordan?" inquired Billy, snickering.

"Her name's Chelsea if you must know, and she isn't my girlfriend. We were just taking her to the hall to show her that it's all changed back to its original state, because for some reason, I don't know why, she doesn't believe us." growled Jordan, his face becoming red from Billy's childish remark.

"You don't have to explain to him about me; I can stick up for myself thank you very much," said Chelsea, glaring over at Billy, arms folded across her chest.

Suddenly, Adam and Amy appeared from behind one of the weather-beaten stone monuments, causing Chelsea to step back in alarm.

"Flaming hell, how many more of you are hiding in here?" she asked, her face glazed with shock.

"Don't be alarmed. There's only the six of us. These two are the ones I mentioned to you back in your kitchen, the brother and sister who disappeared all those years ago," said Jordan, now hoping she may believe him.

*I must be dreaming, and I hope I'll wake up soon,* she thought, shaking her head.

"What was that you said, Jordan? I don't remember you mentioning anything about a brother and sister going missing years ago when we were all in the kitchen," roared Thomas, his breath catching in his throat. "What are you hiding from me, Jordan?" Thomas was now becoming upset, not knowing the full facts about Adam and Amy.

"I updated Chelsea about Adam and Amy when you went to the bathroom, as I didn't want to frighten you. I'm sorry, Thomas; let's just leave it at that for the moment, please?" Jordan was already feeling embarrassed and upset with himself for getting them in this pickle in the first place; he just hoped Thomas didn't probe any further.

Thomas begrudgingly accepted Jordan's apology, as he didn't really want to know the details. He was scared . . . *very* scared . . .

"Let's not hang around here too long. We need to get back to the hall before the sun rises, or else we'll be here for another four years, and I have definitely no designs on that happening, so come on," ordered Jordan, gesturing with his hand for them to follow him.

Jordan was now regretting coming to the hall. "It was a stupid dare anyway," he muttered under his breath once he'd stepped away from James and Thomas.

## Chapter Twenty-Five

Ensuring no one was left behind; the group trudged along the winding, snow-covered path of the cemetery toward the exit, which was positioned at the top of the hill, wondering whether they were going to get back home safely or not. The snow danced and swirled around them. It still remained in deep slushy piles, but in the places where it had not been so thick, dark muddy patches showed.

"Look Chelsea, over there. The hall and the lodge are back to normal; now do you believe us?" yelled Jordan, pointing across at the two buildings.

Chelsea brushed past the six of them to get a clearer view of the hall and lodge. Her mouth dropped open, and she stood rooted to the spot, surveying the unbelievable image before her.

The hall and its surroundings appeared to be bathed in the silver glow of the moon.

"Are you having a laugh? I suppose you think this is funny? Argh! I knew there was something not right about you all. You've been lying to me all along! I've a good mind to drag you all back home. Don't you come anywhere near my family or me ever again," screamed an angry Chelsea, turning on her heels, fighting her way through the thick snow.

"Can't you see what we're seeing, you stupid girl?" screamed James at the retreating figure of Chelsea. An awful feeling slowly crept over his whole body, causing him to shiver.

"Get away, all of you," she shouted over her shoulder as she was trying to control her anger.

*This, I don't like,* thought Jordan, quickly coming to the conclusion that because Chelsea wasn't on the grounds of the hall when the church bells struck midnight, she wouldn't be able to see the effect the rest of them were witnessing.

The group was stunned by Chelsea's surprising observations. The uncertainty of not knowing what to do next made them all drift aimlessly around, trying to come to terms with the fact that they may all be trapped for another four years.

Casting one last frightened and puzzled glance at Chelsea, Billy eventually brought them out of their troubled thoughts.

"Jordan, while we were drifting around the cemetery, and freezing to death, may I add, Amy said she may have remembered what the old man had said to her about the secret to finding a way of getting out of here. And another thing, we accidentally stumbled across a weird looking gravestone with some strange words chiseled into it. It seems to have the remains of a Rebus T. Bones. It may be an ancestor of those two weirdos back at the hall. Well, none of us could make out what the words meant. You three may be able to come up with an answer," Billy suggested. "Do you want to listen to what Amy has to say? You know what, Jordan? I've got a hunch that if we can somehow interpret the words on the gravestone, combined with what Amy comes up with, it may be the key to what we've been searching for, a way of getting us out of this horrible mess. Anyway, that's normally how the good guys end up escaping in most horror books I've read." Billy was praying he was correct.

"Are you certain you can recall all the words, Amy?" asked Jordan, his fingers tightly crossed behind his back.

"Yes, I think so. I'll give it a try anyway," she replied.

"Good luck, Amy, because we certainly need plenty of that at the moment," commented James, drifting closer to her, making certain he could hear every word.

Amy began to concentrate hard, her mind mulling over what the old man had mentioned all those years ago. She just hoped she could remember it all correctly, and in the right order.

Stopping, and closing her eyes, she tried to cast her mind back to when she first heard the old man say those important words. Suddenly, she looked up and stared into the starry sky, speaking out loud for all to hear.

"'Seek out the ones with no voice . . . for they may show you the way.' That's it! I remembered, I remembered," cried Amy, tears streaming down her cheeks.

The rest of the group stood rigid, staring at one another, trying to work out what the words meant, yet none of them could make any sense of them. They were all shocked and bewildered, realizing that they were still in the same predicament they were in a few minutes ago.

It was James who thought he might have solved the riddle.

"I think I may have an idea what the words mean," claimed James, hoping he was correct, as he didn't want to let the group down. "Who do we know that doesn't have a voice . . . shall I give you a clue?" James asked, now feeling more confident.

"James, don't fool around. We haven't got time for playing stupid games; we need to be getting out of here, and soon. Just tell us. Please," urged Jordan.

"Okay, listen up. Dead people don't have a voice, do they? So those strange words on Mr. Rebus T. Bones' grave may 'show us the way.' Am I right, or am I right?" shouted James, certain that he was right.

"I think he may have got it, Jordan," stated Billy, pulling his cap down, shielding his eyes from a sudden gust of wind. "And if I remember correctly from a recent history lesson we had about the mysteries of the pyramids in Egypt; 'Rebus' actually means 'a puzzle in words,'" continued Billy, at the same time giving James a high five. "And I bet that's surprised you all? I do listen now and again to what the teacher has to say in class when it's something I'm interested in," Billy added, grinning over at Thomas.

"Well done, both of you . . . come on then, what are we waiting for? There's only one way to find out. Let's all take a look at these words. Also, I can't think of any other way of getting out of this fiasco," proposed Jordan. "But stay close together," he ordered, feeling downhearted, remembering his promise to his Mum and Dad to look after his two younger brothers.

Wrapping their arms around each other in a cozy little group, the band of warriors cautiously made the long monotonous trek back to the cemetery, and all were hoping that James and Billy were correct.

The weather had suddenly turned colder; the wind was beginning to blow the light dusting of snow around in the air, causing high drifts to stack up on the path and against the walls, which made the long slog back to the cemetery take a little bit longer than expected. This was the reason Jordan sneaked a look over to the east, checking out if the sun was beginning to appear. Luckily, it was still dark in that direction, which caused him to sigh with relief.

Returning to the cemetery, Billy carefully guided the group toward the headstone he'd mentioned.

"James, can we use your flashlight? We can't afford

to be wasting any time trying to read the words in the dark," said Jordan, glancing across at him.

Pulling his hand free from his coat pocket, James happily showed the flashlight to the rest of the group. He switched it on and ran the beam slowly along the chiseled letters, pausing now and again to give them enough time to run their eyes over the words.

"Can anyone make out what the words mean?" asked an anxious looking Thomas, sliding his fingers along the roughly grooved letters.

"Not really, most of them seem to have been worn away," answered James, accepting the fact that they may be trapped here for four more years, tears beginning to form in his eyes.

"Here, let me take proper look, and stop moving the beam around so much, James, I can't see a blinking thing," remarked Jordan, kneeling down, carefully examining the worn out letters.

*Free be present you to back for ard g to depart y u as reverse the take colli shadows two When.*

"Some of the letters seem to be missing," Jordan commented, studying the words.

"What's a Freebe present?" asked Thomas, looking dumbfounded.

"It doesn't say a 'Freebe present,' silly. It says, 'Free be present,'" laughed Jordan, shielding his eyes from the snow, which had begun to start again.

"Never mind colli shadows, I've got the colli

wobbles," giggled James. His witticism caused the rest of the group to start to titter, lifting all their spirits — slightly.

"Cut it out, will you? We can't be loitering about here all night; we need to get back inside the hall. I think that's the only way we are going to get out of this mess," said Jordan, once the laughter had died down.

"Yes, you're right, Jordan," agreed Billy. "The sooner we get back in there, the quicker we'll get out." Billy had to smile when he'd realized what he had just said. *Not to worry,* he thought. *No one else picked up on my stupid remark.*

After a few minutes, they decided it was a complete waste of time to hang around the cemetery trying to decipher some stupid words, which as far as they were concerned may not be the answer to getting out of this nightmare. They lifted themselves up off the snow-covered grave, dusted themselves off, and waded through the thick snow toward the gates, all feeling downhearted.

Snow fell from the inky sky, and the temperature was falling. Ice began to settle on the tall marble monuments, and icicles hung from the telephone wires. Yet, with grim faces, they slowly slogged their way toward the hall, and hopefully to freedom.

"Don't forget, keep your wits about you and stay together. We can't be having any of you wandering off," shuddered Jordan, trying to clear an easy path for them to follow.

"There you go again, Jordan, repeating Dad's sayings. What's the other one he likes to say? Oh yes, 'He's not backward in coming forward,'" howled Thomas, playfully tapping James on the head.

# Chapter Twenty-Six

Jordan suddenly stopped in his tracks, resulting in the ones directly behind him colliding into his back. He glanced back over his shoulder at Thomas, smiling, realizing the importance of Thomas's flippant remark.

"Thomas? You're a blooming genius. I think you may have solved the riddle," roared Jordan, his eyes brimming with joy.

"Have I? What do you mean, Jordan?" queried Thomas, looking mystified.

"I thought there was something odd with the way we were trying to translate the words. What we have to do is read the riddle backward. Come on, let's get back to the cemetery," cried Jordan, looking up into the horizon, noticing, to his horror, that it was getting a shade lighter over in the east. He didn't make any comment to the others, as he didn't want to scare them.

They hurriedly marched in single file, retracing their steps back to the cemetery before heading straight over to the headstone, brushing away the dust and snow from the eroded letters.

"James, come over here and point the flashlight at

the headstone so we can read the words properly," said Jordan, now feeling more confident.

*Free be present you to back for ard g to depart y u as reverse the take colli shadows two When.*

"Read the words backward," urged Jordan, staring at the crowd of bewildered faces around him. "And has anyone got any paper and a pencil? We need to write the words down correctly so we don't get them mixed up."

"Squirrel to the rescue again," shouted James, waving a creased sheet of paper and a small pencil in his hand, which he'd magically produced from the inside of his coat pocket.

"Always the secret squirrel. Well done," said Jordan. "You write the words down as I read them out, okay, James?"

"Okay." replied James, knowing that his obsession with keeping odd things in his pockets may have once again saved the day.

"When two shadows colli . . . any suggestions?" asked Jordan, waiting for a reply.

"Collide," called out Thomas, blinking away the snow from his eyelids.

"Well done, Tom," they all cried out.

"When two shadows collide, take the reverse as you depart to go . . . " Jordan paused, as he couldn't make out the rest of the words.

"I know what it says. Listen up and be quiet," ordered Thomas. "'When two shadows collide, take the reverse as you depart to go forward, back to your present, be free.' Yippee!" yelled Thomas, knowing full well that he had managed to solve the riddle all by himself.

"Wow!" said Jordan. "'Well done, Tom!"

"He may have solved the riddle, but what does it mean?" asked a totally dejected Billy.

"I think I may have an idea," muttered Amy, who'd been listening intently to the discussion.

"The only way we can get back to *our* time is when the sun begins to rise in the east, and the moon starts to slowly sink behind the horizon. It's referring to the sun and moon's shadows colliding. But as far as what 'take the reverse as you depart to go forward' means, I've got no idea. Let's just hope there's nothing else we have to do to get us back home."

"Jordan? I've just been thinking," commented James. "And I don't want any wise cracks from any of you, got it?" he added, smiling over at his friends. "When it says 'as you depart to go forward,' do you think 'depart' means we have to leave the hall as we entered through the front door? And 'forward', means we then go back to the year we came from?"

"I think he may have the answer, guys . . . anyway, what have we got to lose?" said Billy, scanning the frozen faces around him, trying to work out the meaning of the other puzzling words.

"As you've already said, we've got nothing to lose. So come on, what are we waiting for? I would strongly suggest we all concentrate hard. Try and remember what you did when you first entered the hall. I realize it's going to be a lot harder for you two, as you've been here a long time," said Jordan, glancing over in Adam and Amy's direction. "But please try, as we all want to get back to our parents, DON'T WE?" called out an excited Jordan.

"YES, WE DO!" came the unanimous reply, and Billy tossed his cap up in the air.

Stealthily, the small band of troopers advanced toward the hall. They were all concentrating hard, trying to recall what they did when they entered the hall.

"Because we think we have to leave the hall by the front door, I would suggest we don't go in that way, as it may cause the riddle not to work," said Adam, "That's if you all came through that way?"

Billy decided to keep his mouth shut, as it seemed that he was the only one who didn't enter through the front door. He thought he would wait awhile before raising the issue with the rest of them.

"Well, there's no point in making the situation any worse than it already is, so we will take your advice and try another way in," suggested Jordan, after considering other options.

"Thomas, as a matter of interest, how did you manage to get out of the cellar?" asked Jordan.

## Chapter Twenty-Seven

"I don't think going back into the hall my way would be such a good idea . . . I ended up down in the smelly sewers, which was infested with rats, cockroaches, and freezing dirty water. Ugh!" shivered Thomas, remembering his near-death experience and the cold, damp tunnels.

The rest of them looked on in disgust, after taking in the watered down description of his scary adventure.

"If you are all in agreement, I suggest we *do* go through the sewers. At least Thomas can show us the way without getting lost, I hope?" proposed Jordan. "Tom, once we're down there, will you be able to remember your way back to the cellar?" asked Jordan, praying Thomas was going to say yes.

"I think I should be able to. It's really dark and creepy," replied Thomas. Sweat was beginning to form on the palms of his hands, as he wasn't all that enthusiastic about going back down inside the tunnels.

"I'm in, if you all are," piped up James, scanning the worried looking faces around him.

A few nervous seconds passed before they all agreed

it was the only safe solution under the circumstances. So they carried on in silence, plowing through the thick snow, the hoods on their coats becoming coated with the persistent snowfall.

Some few minutes later, they ended up by the gate to the hall. Jordan gestured with his hand for them to stop and then scanned the immediate area, making sure none of the children or the twins were hiding in any of the bushes or sneakily creeping up on them. Satisfied it was safe to move on, he waved his hand for them to gather around him.

"It seems to be quiet and safe for the time being, so let's try and find the opening to the sewers, okay?" Jordan said, staring over at Thomas.

"Thomas, we'll follow you. You're in charge now," ordered James as he moved to one side to let Thomas through to the front of the line.

"If I remember correctly, I . . . think . . . the . . . opening . . . should . . . be . . . just . . . over . . . here . . . somewhere," stammered Thomas, stooping slightly and examining the ground in front of him. The rest of them tagged along behind, scanning the snow-covered ground.

Because Thomas was having a hard time locating the opening, the rest of the group slumped heavily down in the snow, moaning and complaining about having to hang around in the cold. This only pressured Thomas into hurrying up. They also reminded him it was getting close to sunrise.

"Thomas, we haven't got all night, or should I say all morning? Where's the entrance? It's beginning to get light on the horizon!" shouted Jordan, suddenly becoming desperate.

"Don't shout at me, Jordan. I'm trying as hard as I can. It's not easy, you know, especially with you all watching over me," moaned Thomas, kneeling down, sweeping the snow to one side with his cold, wet hands.

"Look, you all stay over there while I help Thomas," suggested Jordan. "And can I borrow your flashlight, James? It may help us. The light around here isn't all that good to see what we're doing."

Leaving the fidgety group, Thomas guided Jordan over to where he thought the opening might be located.

An anxious five minutes later, Thomas finally found the manhole cover; much to his relief.

"Here it is, Jordan!" cried Thomas, waving his hand around in the air.

"Billy, James, over here, all of you! Thomas has finally found the entrance, and we're running out of time; we need to get back inside the hall as soon as possible," called out Jordan, gesturing to them to move quickly.

Lifting themselves off the cold, damp floor, brushing away the snow from the seat of their pants, the four freezing, relieved, and happy children ran over toward Jordan and Thomas. After all the backslapping and praises were over, the group of six circled the manhole cover, waiting nervously for someone to make the first move.

"Billy, position yourself over on that side of the manhole cover, while I stand here, and when we're certain we have a firm enough grip to lift it, I'll whisper, 'Go!' Okay, Billy?" asked Jordan, waiting for a reply.

"Yes, ready when you are, Waldron," replied Billy, inching his way closer to Jordan.

Certain they were all set to go, Jordan gave the order to lift. Ensuring their knees were bent, they carefully lifted the cover and dragged it over to one side, leaving enough space around the opening for them to climb down. One by one, they curiously came over to peer down into the depths of the sewer, causing them to shiver and step away from the revolting smell drifting up toward them. It was only Thomas who knew what to expect, once they were down there, in the dark . . .

Switching on his flashlight, James began to point the beam down into the opening, making sure that none of the nasty children were down there waiting for them.

Satisfied the coast was clear, the five boys and one girl prepared themselves to climb down the rickety ladder with the distinctive sounds of scurrying feet echoing in the crisscrossing tunnels below them, leaving the children to wonder what they had gotten themselves into. Thomas had mentioned earlier to Jordan and Billy about the unstable ladder, suggesting that one of them should stay at the top to hold on to it, preventing it from falling away from the brickwork. Jordan and Billy agreed to Thomas's suggestion, leaving Billy to stay at the top until they were all safely down.

It took fifteen hard, exhausting, and anxious minutes to reach the wet floor safely.

# Chapter Twenty-Eight

Satisfied none of the dirty children or either of the twins was prowling around, the small band of bedraggled soldiers cautiously traipsed along behind Thomas through the winding, damp tunnels, following the curves of the stone walls, which, to their disgust, were dripping with stagnant water. It felt cold down in the tunnels, yet sweat was forming on their brows, and they were all shivering due to the draft that had suddenly sprung up. The persistent echo of water dripped from the tunnel's curved brick ceiling, combining with the sounds of splashing from their cautious footsteps.

"It stinks down here, and I don't like the sound that's coming from up there," cried James; a steady stream of brown water covering his already soaked sneakers.

"Point the beam further into the tunnel, James; let's see if we can spot what's up ahead. We don't want any surprises," suggested Billy, stepping closer to James.

The beam probed the darkness of the passageways, the faint light picking out the glimmer of pools of stagnant water in front of them. They could hear skittering sounds up ahead, the pattering of vermin feet and the steady metronome-like drip, drip, drip of moisture from the curved tunnel roof above them.

"Oh crap, the battery running out in my flashlight. You'll have to be extra careful where you put your hands and feet now," moaned James, slapping the flashlight on the palm of his hand, hoping to bring some life back into it.

"Thomas, will you light one of your candles? We need some kind of light back here to see where we're going. We don't want to bump into any of you," called out Billy from the back of the line. Billy had volunteered to stand guard, watching out for anything or anyone who may sneak up on them from behind, which made him feel brave. Also, he felt as though he was doing something important for the friends he had just made.

They had barely taken ten steps before James shouted for them to stop. "I can feel the floor and walls vibrating around us; can you feel it as well?" he asked, holding on to the side of the tunnel for some means of support, screwing his eyes up, trying to see into the fading darkness.

"Oh! Oh! It's that filthy water from the last time I was down here. Quickly, all of you grab hold of something, and make sure you lift your feet well away from the floor, or else you will be swept away. And if there are any broken branches in the rushing water, make sure you keep well away from them, as they may pull you in," cried Thomas, desperately searching for something to grab onto, as he didn't want to experience the distress and fear again.

Within seconds of them finding some kind of handhold or ledge to climb onto, a whoosh of cold air assaulted them. Then, approaching them fast, like a speeding truck, a giant bank of freezing water rolled toward them. Hundreds of gallons of putrid cold water came rushing down the twisting tunnels toward the terrified looking children.

"Close your eyes, and look away from the water so it won't go up your nose and in your mouth!" screamed Thomas above the roar of the water; seconds before it reached them.

They were all hanging on for dear life to anything they could find.

After thirty seconds of mayhem and a good soaking, the rampaging water stopped as suddenly as it had started, leaving the children to let out an almighty sigh of relief. They readjusted their wet clothes, staring at the diminishing filthy water down the tunnel.

"Is everybody all right? We haven't lost anyone, have we?" yelled Jordan over the fading roar of the water.

"Yes, we're all fine back here, thanks! I don't think anyone's gone missing," came the response, combined with occasional coughing and spluttering coming from the darkness.

"Where's Billy? Can anyone see him?" wailed Amy. "Oh no! He must have been swept away!"

## Chapter Twenty-Nine

"Jordan, is that Billy's cap and jacket over there in the water? Oh no! It's Billy, and he seems to be floating face down! Hurry up! We need to get him out of the water right away!" shouted a panic-stricken James, sloshing his way through the ankle-deep water.

Jordan was the first to reach Billy. He quickly plunged his hand into the icy water, grabbing ahold of the back of his jacket, preparing himself to see Billy's lifeless eyes staring back up at him, making him feel sick to the stomach.

To Jordan's utter astonishment, his hand disappeared beneath the slimy water, along with the jacket he was desperately clinging onto, causing him to lose his balance and land in the shallow foul water up to his knees. After the initial shock of not finding Billy, he heaved himself up, pulling out the soggy jacket and cap for the rest of them to see. The expressions on all their faces were distressed, their mouths hanging open in total shock.

"Whew! I thought I was a goner back there, guys," the croaky voice declared from the inky darkness behind them.

Jordan was the first to notice Billy's shadowy figure staggering toward them, leaning on the damp walls for a means of support. The others turned to stare at him as though they were seeing a ghost.

"Billy, what happened to you? We all thought you'd drowned when we first spotted these floating about in the water," whimpered Jordan, offering the dank, wet, dripping jacket and cap over to Billy.

"I lost my grip on a piece of brickwork I was clinging onto when the rushing water struck me. The next thing I remembered was hearing you all talking. Anyway, I seem to be fine; no broken bones. I'm just soaking wet, that's all, and thanks for worrying about me," said Billy, looking slightly embarrassed by the friendship being shown. Jordan slipped his jacket and sweater off and handed his sweater over to Billy. Billy was stunned by the friendship shown by Jordan, which made him feel guilty for putting them in this situation in the first place.

Having gotten their emotions in check, Thomas squeezed his way through the group to the front, and with some difficulty, fought his way through the slimy water toward what he thought was the opening of the cellar, as he was now anxious to get out of the smelly, wet tunnel.

Carefully forging along, he spied a number of furry, obscure looking remains floating around by his feet. This time he had no intentions of inspecting any of them.

They continued on into the darkness a while longer, occasionally stopping and waiting for Thomas to give them the thumbs-up sign, indicating that they were still going in the right direction.

A sudden movement and a splash made them all jump out of their skins. A sleek, grey object leapt from the black, rippling water and streaked along the ledge by their side. It stopped and studied the group of terrified children before wiping its snout with its paws and flicking its head, sending droplets onto their hair and clothes. It was a large rat with glistening eyes, smooth grey coat, and large, bright pink ears.

After getting their nerves in check, they cautiously headed on down the damp tunnel, where, to their surprise, it split into two. "Where to now?" inquired Jordan, sweat rolling down his ghostly looking face.

Thomas glanced back at their bright eyes gleaming in their grubby faces. "To the left, I'm pretty sure." He knew he was going in the right direction when he'd spotted the remains of the floating furry creature he'd come across before.

"I hope you're right, Tom, or else we're going to be trapped down here for ages," commented Jordan, releasing a pent-up breath.

Like a hungry mouth, the dark, unwelcoming tunnel swallowed them all . . .

They had only walked for a short period of time when Thomas raised his right hand for them to stop. Gazing up into the inky darkness, he saw a small chink of light coming through the gap of the trapdoor to the cellar.

"Phew!" muttered Thomas under his breath, realizing he had luckily found the way out of the tunnel.

"Well done, Tom," whispered Jordan into Thomas's ear.

Standing at the bottom of the rusty metal ladder that would eventually lead them up to the cellar, Jordan gripped the bottom rung before lifting himself up, heading toward the top, all the while listening out for any movement coming from above.

Reaching the top of the ladder, he slowly lifted the trapdoor a crack before sliding it to one side, peering into the room. To his relief, it was deserted.

Bending down, Jordan whispered for them to follow him up. Aware they had heard him, Jordan began to slide the trapdoor a few feet away from the opening, giving them sufficient space to climb out without any difficulty. One by one, they climbed the rickety ladder, sweat streaming down their dirty faces.

Moments later, they had safely entered the cellar. They stood in the small confines of the room, trying to get their breath back.

"Wait a minute. Have you all remembered what you did when you first came into the hall?" asked Jordan, scanning the concerned faces.

"I think I can," responded Amy.

"Yes, and I think I can as well," said Adam. "I

realize it was years ago, but we don't have any choice in the matter, do we?"

"What about you three?" Jordan asked, staring across at Thomas, James, and Billy.

"I think I can remember. What about you, Tom?" queried James.

"I think so," replied Thomas, trying very hard to cast his mind back to when they came in the hall, becoming frightened that he may have forgotten something.

Billy then chirped up, deciding now was the time to give them the bad news.

"I can't go out through the front door with you all. I came in by the fire door at the top of the building, remember? I'll have to make my own way up there once we are safely back in the kitchen," said Billy, walking away with his head down, aware that he would have to leave his newfound friends.

"I'm sorry, Billy, but you're right, and if you want to get out of here, you've got no other choice. Don't worry, we'll all be waiting for you outside, won't we?" remarked Jordan, looking across at the rest of them, who echoed, "Yes."

Agreeing that was the best course of action, they cautiously crept toward the elevator, hoping Scally hadn't done anything to prevent it from being used.

Jordan was the first to arrive. He craned his neck up into the shaft, checking if there were any voices or sounds of shuffling feet high above him in the kitchen.

"Thomas, it seems as though your quick thinking with the kitchen utensils certainly worked. Well done, Tom," smiled Jordan, hugging him tightly.

"I'm not as thick as you all think I am, am I?" commented Thomas with a smile, glancing over at Billy.

"Listen up, guys, there doesn't seem to be anyone up there at the moment, so I suggest we send Billy up first. That way, while he's assisting me with the pulling of the ropes from the top, he can listen out for any movement outside in the corridor, and if anyone does appear, he will be able to warn us. We'll send Amy and Adam up next, followed by James and Thomas. I'd be best going up last, as we'll need someone down here who will be strong enough to pull on the ropes. Agreed?" Jordan asked, chewing his bottom lip.

"Good idea, Jordan," said Billy, his dirty face brightening up.

"What time is it, Jordan?" inquired James, becoming worried they may be running out of time.

"I've got no idea, James. Have you forgotten that my watch is broken and my cell phone is utterly useless? Let's not dwell on it now; the most important thing at the moment is for us to get out of the cellar and then the kitchen. Come on, Billy, get yourself positioned properly in the elevator so you can be on your way," ordered Jordan, taking Thomas's two kitchen tools away from the dangling ropes.

## Chapter Thirty

Once Billy had hoisted himself up into the elevator, and made himself as comfortable as possible in the cramped space, Jordan and James positioned themselves at both sides of the elevator, tightly gripping the ropes. Then slowly, inch-by-inch, they proceeded to pull Billy up the short distance to the kitchen.

"I've made it safely, guys; you can stop pulling now. And the kitchen's deserted," shouted Billy. "Just let me know when you're sending the next one up, okay?" he said, tilting his head over the shaft.

"Billy, Amy's in the elevator. Are you ready?"

"Yes," came the reply.

It took fifteen sweaty, tiring minutes to get them all safely up the elevator; leaving Jordan flaked out on the floor of the kitchen, gasping for breath.

"Are you all right, Jordan?" asked a worried Thomas, concern in his voice.

"Y-e-e-s," gasped Jordan, "just give me a few minutes t-o-o get m-y breath b-a-a-c-k, will you?"

While Jordan was slowly trying to get his breathing back to normal, Billy began to wonder how he was going to get upstairs to the top of the hall, especially having to creep past the many rooms and landings on the way, which no doubt would have the children and the terrible twins hiding inside.

He then came up with a brilliant idea.

"Jordan, there is no way I'm going be able to get past that group up there. So if the four of you work together on the ropes, you should be able to pull me up to the top of the building in the elevator. That way I may be able to find the room with the fire door, and escape down the fire escape. What do you think?" inquired Billy, now becoming eager to get out.

"Smart idea, Billy," said Jordan enthusiastically. "Come on, guys, start looking around for a cloth to wrap your hands around. We don't want you to end up with blisters all over your palms,"' he suggested, frantically searching for something in the drawers and on top of the dusty shelves.

As James was rummaging through one of the drawers, the little mouse that was nestled in his shirt began to stir, causing him to chuckle and jiggle around as though he had fleas.

"What's so funny, James?" asked Thomas, a look of surprise across his filthy face.

"Nothing. I just had a tickle on my tummy, that's all," replied James, delicately positioning the mouse back into the folds of his shirt.

"You'd best check inside your shirt and sweater,

James. You never know, you may have a spider hidden in there from the tunnels or the cellar," giggled Thomas.

James ignored his brother's comment, and carried on searching the room for something to wrap around his cold, shivering hands.

Happy that everyone had some means of protection, Billy shook their hands, thanked Jordan for all his help, and apologized for getting him into this mess in the first place.

Jordan replied by saying, "No problem; that's what friends are for." This caused Billy to turn away in embarrassment, trying to hold back a lump in his throat.

With everyone ready, willing, and able, Billy began to hoist himself up into the cramped elevator. Then, to their horror, they heard a door slam somewhere in the building, and the unnerving sound of pounding feet.

## Chapter Thirty-One

"Jordan, it seems as though we haven't got much time," observed Billy, sweat beading on his face. "If Scally and the rest of the children end up blocking the downstairs corridor to the front door, you all are going to have a hard time getting out of the hall. What we need is a distraction, and I may have the answer. When I was roaming round the grounds last night, I noticed a number of bats entering and leaving the eaves at the top of the building. I'll try and find a way into the loft. I don't think it will be that difficult. Hopefully, I can spook them and get them to fly down into the hallway. That may give you the time and opportunity you need to get out of here. Agreed?"

"Secret squirrel to the rescue again," chipped in James, who'd be listening with interest to Billy's suggestion.

While they were all wondering what James was talking about, he pulled his hand out from his coat pocket only to reveal, to their astonishment, half a dozen indoor fireworks resting on the palms of his hands.

"Where did you find those, James?" asked Jordan, a look of surprise on his face.

"I kept a few back from the New Year's Eve party; you'd be surprised what I store in my pockets," laughed James, carefully inspecting the fireworks, ensuring the ends were dry and intact.

"I don't think any of us want to know what you keep in your pockets, but anyway, well done, James; once again you've come to our rescue. Let's just hope they all work," stated Jordan. "And I think I may have some matches left from the lodge," he said, searching through the pockets of his jacket.

"I have some too — look," interrupted Thomas, revealing the box of matches.

"Great! Billy, you take three of the fireworks, along with my matches, and we'll keep the rest, okay?" suggested Jordan. "And all of you be quiet; we don't want any of them upstairs to know what we're up to."

"We need to use these to our advantage," he continued. "It may be best if you set off your fireworks first to frighten the bats, and when we hear the explosions going off, we'll set off ours. That way, Scally and the rest of them will be so confused; they won't know what's happening around them. Are we all agreed?"

They all nodded their agreement, and once they had wished each other the best of luck, they began to haul Billy up in the elevator, not knowing what was happening upstairs and in the corridor. At that precise moment, it was all quiet, much to their relief. Or was it?

"I think they've all disappeared; it seems deathly

quiet out there," whispered James, licking his dry lips.

"They haven't. I can see at least six children and that obnoxious Scally loitering near the front door," sputtered Amy as she slyly peered around the edge of the splintered doorframe.

"Amy, for crying out loud, move away from there this second! If we're lucky, we may get away with this," fumed Jordan, grinding out the words between clenched teeth.

Amy quickly moved away from the door, feeling annoyed with herself for doubting Jordan's word and knowing he was only trying to help them all.

Confident that Scally and the other children weren't about to come and check out the kitchen, the four boys began to pull hard on both sets of ropes. It didn't take long for Billy to reach the top of the building. He then called down to inform them that he had arrived safely, and he wished them all good luck. The group echoed back their sentiments.

The remaining five shuffled in a little closer to each other for comfort and support, nervously waiting for the explosions to begin, which they knew would take place any moment.

"How much longer, Jordan?" asked a nervous Thomas, the stress now showing on his young, innocent face.

"I'd guess a couple of minutes, that's all," replied Jordan, affectionately embracing him.

"This is going to work, isn't it, Jordan?" piped up James, who had sidled closer toward his brother.

"Sure. It's going to be fine, you just wait and see," answered an unconvincing Jordan.

## Chapter Thirty-Two

While the five of them were patiently waiting downstairs in the kitchen, Billy had clambered out of the elevator and within seconds had found the door leading to the loft. He was trying his best to be as quiet as possible, as he didn't want to disturb the sleeping bats too soon. He wanted the whole effect of the exploding fireworks to be as spectacular and stunning as possible.

Stealthily crouching down and crawling on his hands and knees, he noticed dark and rank bat droppings coating the floor and lodged in between the dust-laden wooden joists of the loft. His eyes began to sting from the putrid smell rising from the floor. He had to be extra careful, as he didn't want to slip and fall through the flimsy plastered ceiling.

Eventually arriving by the trapdoor in the loft, he slowly lifted it up and peered down from a dizzying height into the main hall below. To his surprise and relief, he was looking straight down into the corridor, which led to the hallway where his friends were to make their escape. He then suddenly spied Scally, along with a number of dirty children, hanging around the front door, which gave him some concerns.

*Never mind,* he thought, cheekily. *Once the explosions start, that should give the others the opportunity to get out of the hall.*

He carefully eased the trapdoor open as far as it would go before clearing away as many cobwebs and bat droppings from around the opening as possible, making sure the bats didn't have any obstructions while fleeing from the loft. He then settled himself down cross-legged on the rancid smelly floor, well away from the mouth of the hole, as he didn't want the leathery winged flying animals to end up in his hair. Carefully pulling out the fireworks and matches from his coat pocket, he prepared himself for some serious, wicked excitement.

There must be at least a hundred bats hanging from the loft beams up here, guessed Billy, smiling, knowing when they started to bolt through the opening, the bats and the shock of the explosions would automatically confuse Scally and the children guarding the entrance to the hall. *Let's hope it gives Jordan and the rest of them enough time to get out,* he thought.

"Oh, boy . . . this had better work," shuddered Billy, the awful stench of bat droppings irritating his nose.

Within seconds of the fireworks exploding and snapping within the small cooped up loft, dozens of sleepy bats took flight from the beams and rafters, down toward the landing and the hallway below. They were all trying desperately to squeeze through the small opening of the loft. The tumultuous noise engulfing Billy was deafening. He quickly covered his ears with his hands, and the draft from the bats' frantic flapping wings caused the layers of dust and cobwebs to end up plastered all over Billy's face and hair, which he quickly wiped away with the palms of his hands.

Down below in the kitchen, Jordan and the rest of the group were waiting patiently by the broken kitchen door. Then, to their sheer delight, there was the sudden ear-splitting sound of firecrackers and pops that could be heard all over the corridors and hallways around the massive hall. Above the explosions and popping, they could also make out the sounds of dozens of fluttering wings. Within seconds, the hallways, corridors, and landings were full of bats, all frantically trying to find a way out of the building.

"Keep your heads down and cover your faces," Scally yelled above the noise. The other children howled in panic while Scally remained rooted to the spot, mesmerized by the spectacle of the hurtling, careening animals flying around him.

Within seconds, the air was thick with frenzied bats, too numerous to count. It was like a swarm of angry wasps. They skirted past and around them so quickly that Scally and the other children couldn't keep track of a single one of them. Leather wings thrummed currents of dusty air around their heads as the bats began to plunge at them, swerving aside at the last moment.

Jordan then set off his fireworks, the bats suddenly turning tail and flying back to where they originally came from. In the meantime, the children in the corridor were still frantically trying to cover their faces with their hands and arms from all the bats that were by now becoming crazed and frightened, causing the bats to swoop in and out of any of the rooms were the doors had been left open. Scally instructed the children to follow him up the stairs, where he hoped it would be safer. Jordan duly noted this.

Aware that the opportunity for them to escape had finally arrived, he instantly ordered James, Thomas, Amy, and Adam to carefully make their way to the front door.

"Walk backward when we go out of the front door. That may help us. We must go out the way we came in, and walking backward may be the last clue to the riddle," James informed them, while keeping a close eye on the bats that were flying manically all over the place.

"Good thinking, James. I think you may be correct. Keep your heads down. Are you all ready?" called out Jordan, sweating and panting for breath. "And don't forget to walk backwards."

"Ready, and we won't forget, Jordan!" they all shouted above the noise of the bats.

Ensuring they weren't going to fall over in the

commotion that was going on all around them, all five moved backward down the long corridor toward the front door, ducking and stumbling along, frantically trying to avoid the swooping bats, which were now becoming berserk and distraught.

In the midst of all this nightmarish confusion going on around him, Jordan glanced behind just in time to see a particularly large bat hurtle straight into the back of Thomas's head, ending up caught in the hood of Thomas's jacket. He heard the soft thud as it struck him. The collision sent Thomas sprawling. Jordan raced over to help Thomas, trying to protect his own face with his arm, and at the same time grappling with the bat. After frantically struggling with the bat, Jordan somehow managed to release it from Thomas's hood before tossing it into the air.

Shouting, he pulled Thomas to his feet, and although slightly dazed and running unsteadily, Jordan guided him closer the front door. Amy and Adam were also lashing out, trying to ward off the flying beasts. They were all just a moist blur before their stinging eyes.

Seconds later, Amy and Adam found themselves by the front door, exhausted but relieved. With an almighty push, they managed to ease the door open, quickly exiting the hall, disappearing into the darkness. James soon followed, as all three had successfully remembered what they did when they originally entered the hall all those years and hours ago.

Yet Jordan and Thomas were being held back, due to the dozens of confused bats that were preventing them moving any further down the congested corridor. They heard several bangs and squealing coming from some of the bats as they collided against the closed doors and walls.

Through all the commotion and the deafening noise that was going on around them inside, an unexpected loud, piercing cry was heard from the outside. It was Amy.

"Jordan, it's starting to get light out here! The sun's coming up! Hurry up! Can you hear me in there?" Amy's frantic raving faded in the morning air due to the pandemonium that was going on inside.

Outside, dawn was slowly breaking in the east. The sun was burning away the early morning snow clouds, resulting in the sun's rays to sweep along the vast white landscape in the distance. In a few minutes time, those rays would eventually overlap the moon's fading shadow, causing the hall and grounds to be returned to its old decrepit state, leaving Jordan and Thomas trapped inside for four years. That is, unless they managed to fight their way to the front door, and freedom.

# Chapter Thirty-Three

Minutes later, the sun's rays began to creep across the roof of the building. The outside walls began to shudder and collapse in stages, triggering the roof tiles to fly off, crashing down to the snow-covered ground before exploding into thousands of tiny sharp projectiles shooting off in all directions. The walls in the many rooms upstairs were beginning to implode on themselves, causing an avalanche of plaster to fall down, bringing a large section of the wall toppling down, colliding one into another like dominoes in a chain reaction, raising a thick dust of debris to float around the corridors and hallways. The ground itself rocked with each impact. A large section of fractured column slammed into the ground. All the windows began to rattle in their frames from the vibrations of the building, causing the glass to shatter. Shards of tiny pieces of glass tinkled down like crystal snow, sparkling like gems. The whole building began to shake and sway like a tree in a tropical storm, resulting in the two large glass chandeliers in the main hallway to rattle and swing from side to side. Eventually, they both came away from their mountings before crashing down onto the wooden floor, exploding into thousands of tiny sharp fragments, sending a dust of powdered glass into the dusty air, clogging Jordan and Thomas's throats and stinging their eyes.

As all of this was going on around them, Jordan and Thomas had quickly sprinted over to the large curtain by the entrance, which fortunately for them, was still hanging by a small number of curtain hooks. They quickly wrapped it around their trembling bodies, hoping it would protect them from the flying glass and debris that was being jettisoned from all directions from the collapsing walls and erupting floor.

It was then that Jordan realized what was happening around him.

"The hall's starting to revert back to its old decrepit state; we need to get out of here right now! How do you feel, Thomas? Are you all right to run?" asked Jordan, picking out fragments of glass from their hair, and dusting them both down from the thick layer of plaster that covered their whole bodies.

Thomas rubbed the back of his head. There was no evidence of blood on the palm of his hand, so he nodded and gestured for Jordan to move.

"Ha ha! Look around you little boys; we've got you both now. It's too late; you won't be able to get out now," bellowed the old man, who throughout all the havoc, had been crouched down, taking cover at the top of the stairs from the bats and flying glass. Huddled along side him were his sister, together with Scally.

Jordan stood transfixed, staring up at the old man's manic face, and spotting some activity in the uppermost part of the landing, just by the wooden cross-beams. Then, to his astonishment, thousands of spiders were being violently shaken out of their webs and cascading down around the group that was huddled on top of the landing. Within seconds, the dirty children were frantically pounding their feet up and down on the floor which by now was covered with big black gruesome looking spiders.

The stair carpet and floorboards resembled a molten black river of spiders as it oozed toward Jordan and Thomas. Hundreds of spiders were crawling all over the walls and around the banisters. Some of them even ended up in the hair of the pursuing children, resulting in them screaming and shaking their heads, trying to rid them of the small black creatures that were hidden deep inside their hair.

Everything going on around Jordan seemed to be in slow motion, and he knew he had to snap out of his trance as soon as possible; if not, he and Thomas would end up being trapped inside the hall. He began to concentrate, shaking his head, hoping to clear it. Thankfully, it worked. Gripping Thomas by the shoulders, he pushed him toward the front door, instructing him to hurry through, which would only leave him to escape.

While all this was happening, Jordan noticed that the destruction of the hall was slowly creeping toward him. Just then, the ground shifted underneath him, shaking violently. The wooden floor creaked and groaned, and there were more loud sounds coming from far below in the cellar. The floor started to shimmer like hot tarmac on a sun-baked road. Tree roots began to sprout up through the floorboards; deep fractures ripped through the floor, causing the wood to splinter and explode, giving the impression of a banana skin being peeled back. The stairs began to sway and creak. The shaking caused the group on the stairs to grab ahold of the handrail and wall for some means of support. The sounds of the shifting timbers could be heard above the racket that engulfed them. Then part of the roof came crashing down around Jordan's feet, which thankfully brought him out of his daze.

"Thomas, move yourself — now! I'll follow you!" hollered Jordan, panicking. Sweat was streaming down his face. Then he noticed, to his horror; Thomas hadn't exited the door yet.

"What are you waiting for, Tom? Get out of here now!" repeated Jordan, hoping Thomas had heard him over the uproar and groaning around him. When he stopped to look back at the scene unfolding around him, he saw an escalating rippling effect coming from the kitchen, spreading out across the floor and walls, causing the dust and debris to rise like a fine floating mist. The air seemed to shimmer. So intense was the flow of energy, the walls began to crack and open up; purple bolts of lightning shot out from all sides, scudding across the floor, crawling along the walls and ceiling — toward Jordan!

Jordan then noticed that the bats had suddenly vanished, and the thousands of spiders had mysteriously disappeared too, which left him to wonder if this was all just a nightmare . . .

Worried that he may not remember everything he did when he entered the hall, Thomas stopped before squeezing his way through to freedom. He then looked up at the smiling door knocker.

"Right! I stroked the gargoyle's nose, and then I crossed my fingers. Was that all?" mumbled Thomas, the raucous sounds sneaking up on him.

"Move it, Thomas, I'm coming out!" screamed Jordan, sprinting toward the door. "Can you hear me, Tom?"

The destruction of the hall was coming to its grisly end. Only the last few feet of the walls and floors were intact, giving Jordan a few desperate minutes before he could make his escape.

Once he was safely outside, Jordan paused to turn back and glance through the small opening of the door at the havoc close behind. He had an awful feeling that something wasn't quite right. *The destruction and chaos should be coming to an end by now,* he thought. *It seems as though we've all managed to get out safely.*

*I just hope they've all remembered what they did when they first came in the hall, especially Billy.*

"Listen, all of you, if we've followed the riddle correctly, we should be safe now and the hall should have stopped collapsing. Did any of you forget something? If you don't come up with the answer soon, we're all going to be stuck here!" hollered Jordan, his whole body shaking with fright, rivulets of sweat evident on his face. He was totally exhausted.

It was when the remaining parts of the collapsing walls and erupting floorboards were just a few feet from the door that Thomas recalled that he had also crossed his eyes when entering the hall.

In an instant, Thomas scurried back to the entrance, squeezing his way through the gap of the door into the corridor. Before he could go any further, his concentration was broken by the movement of a grubby hand suddenly grabbing him by the scruff of his neck, yanking him back into the hall, resulting in Thomas landing heavily on his back.

## Chapter Thirty-Four

Thomas jerked his head around to catch a glimpse of his assailant. In the scant, dusty light, he saw Scally leering down at him.

During all the commotion that had been going on inside the hall, Scally had cleverly managed to fight his way down the shaky fractured staircase by using his grubby T-shirt as a means of wafting away the bats and spiders. There was no way he was going to let all the prisoners get away; he wanted to keep at least one of them back if at all possible.

"JORDAN!" Thomas screamed at the top of his lungs.

Just then, a whole section of the wooden floor where Thomas had just been sitting, fell away, leaving a jagged black hole just inches from his outstretched feet.

Gazing down, Thomas noticed that the hole had a drop of at least one hundred feet into the smelly sewers. Thomas sat there mesmerized, shaking with fear. To his dismay, he noticed that the hole was far too wide for him to jump over or for his brothers to safely reach him.

Then with some effort, Scally eventually managed to drag Thomas along the floor to the foot of the stairs, well away from the dark hole.

As this was going on inside, Jordan and James were wondering what had become of Thomas. Then they heard the guttural scream coming from the inside of the hall.

"That was Thomas! Come on, James!" gasped Jordan, feeling as if someone had wrenched his heart out of his chest.

Barging their way in through the doorway, they saw, to their sheer horror, Thomas sprawled out on the floor at the foot of the ruined stairs, with Scally smirking over at them. The wide crevice spread out in front of them, and they knew immediately that there was no way they would be able to jump across it safely.

Thomas snapped out of his frightened state of mind when he spied Jordan and James staring across at him from the opposite side of the gaping hole.

"Jordan, James, please don't leave me here all by myself!" sobbed Thomas, tears streaming down his cheeks, tracing dark tracks on his chalky face.

Scally still had a firm grip on Thomas's jacket and he was now in the process of hauling him up the rickety stairs.

While Jordan and James were frantically wondering what to do next, another large section of wooden paneling came crashing down to the damaged floor. Luckily, the length was long enough for it to reach the other side of the hole where Thomas was being dragged away up the stairs. All of a sudden a deep rumble could be heard all over the hall, and the floor trembled violently beneath their feet, resulting in Jordan and James crashing down to the dusty floor.

In a flash, James lifted himself up from the floor and sprinted across the wooden paneling to help Thomas, at the same time pulling out a can of Silly String. Within a matter of seconds, he had squirted it all over Scally's face and hair. Scally automatically wiped away the gooey mess with his hands, which released Thomas from his grasp.

Realizing he was free, Thomas jumped to his feet, and along with James's help, dashed across the horizontal wooden paneling.

Unfortunately, due to the combined weight of them both, it began to buckle and bend, so they quickly retraced their steps back to the other side. Just then, one of the heavy wooden beams above them creaked and slid, releasing a large avalanche of dust and debris down on to them.

"James, Tom, can you hear me over there? I'm going to throw the curtain over to you, so grab ahold of it and then use it to help yourself get across the plank! It'd be best if you come over one at a time; that might help. But be quick about it!" screamed Jordan, desperately tugging on the curtain, trying to pull it away from the hooks and hoping they had heard him above the noise that was going on around them.

After the second tug, the curtain fell with a thud to the glass-covered floor, resulting in a cloud of plaster to rise up into the already dusty air.

While all this was going on, James had returned to Scally and was spurting the remains of the Silly String over Scally's already gooey face.

Meanwhile, Thomas was teetering on the edge of the hole, waiting nervously for Jordan to toss the curtain across. Luckily for them, James and Thomas had managed to hear Jordan's frantic instructions above the creaking and rumbling in the hall.

Gripping the heavy curtain with both hands, Jordan spun around a couple of times before releasing a large portion across the gaping, smelly hole and ensuring he had ahold of one end of the curtain. In the meantime, James had left Scally on the stairs spluttering and shouting.

Thomas caught the curtain and was the first to dash across the wooden plank. Behind him, James started to run . . .

Suddenly, the deep rumblings in the hall increased in volume, and the plank fell away from under him.

James screamed, and then the scream was knocked out of him as he fell short, slamming up against the newly exposed edge of the hole.

He clawed at the wooden floorboards with one hand while gripping the curtain with the other, unable to find a foothold.

Jordan leaned on his stomach and grabbed his hand

just as James lost his grip of the curtain. "Thomas!" he gasped as James's weight crushed his wrist against the edge of the splintered floor. "Get yourself over here now and grab his other hand!"

Thomas scrambled over to Jordan, only to see James flailing below. He reached out for his other hand. "James! Here!"

James looked up at them both, terrified. "Please don't let me fall!"

"You're not gonna fall," Thomas promised, as their fingers touched, then slipped apart.

Jordan was losing his hold. "Thomas, come on . . ." he begged.

Thomas dropped to his knees, leaned out over the abyss—and lunged.

This time he caught James's wrist. Straining, almost overbalancing, Thomas hauled him up, taking just enough pressure off Jordan for him to bring around his other arm. "Got him!" Jordan barked. "Pull!"

Leaning back, Thomas pulled with all his strength. Jordan forced himself upright and dragged James up, all three falling in a heap on the rubble that was covering the floor.

Jordan sat up. "You okay?" he asked James.

James whispered, "Thank you," and nodded.

"Good! Now, let's get out of here."

As Scally was finishing wiping away the clammy string from his face, he saw, to his disappointment, the three boys making their escape through the front door. "Never mind," he muttered. "There's always another leap year to look forward to."

"You two go out first," instructed Thomas, pushing Jordan and James through the door. "I can remember now what I did when I first came into the hall."

Once he'd collected his thoughts, Thomas carefully scampered backward over the door's threshold. But this time, he rubbed the door knocker's nose, crossed his fingers . . . and crossed his eyes.

As soon as Thomas had completed all three actions, the hall abruptly reappeared in its old rundown state, exactly like when they first came upon it just a few frightening hours before. The last remnants of dust and plaster poured out of the doorway, and it soon cleared around them, drifting into the chilly morning air.

All of a sudden there was an overpowering wind, a blinding flash of lightening, and a clap of thunder, so loud that it hurt their ears, and they found themselves on their knees in the deep snow.

The hall became a shimmering window of air, leaving it once again with boarded up windows. The razor-wire around the wooden guttering appeared at the top of the hall and the snow-covered path leading up to the hall looked as though it was once again carpeted with thick moss and grass.

James collapsed on the floor, ran his hand over his wet tousled hair, and began to cry, realizing that they had all managed to get out of the hall safely.

"I nearly had an accident in my pants back there. Thanks, guys, for saving me . . . and where have Adam and Amy gone to?" chuckled James, scanning the area, which was beginning to lighten up from the early morning sun.

"They must have become frightened and decided to make their way home, which doesn't surprise me. But I'm upset that they didn't stay back long enough to thank us all for getting them out," giggled Jordan. "Come on, let's not worry about them. As long as we're safe, that's all that matters. Let's head for home."

"Do you think Billy managed to get out of the hall in time? Has anyone seen him?" asked Thomas, reliving the past few hours, causing him to shiver.

"I haven't seen him," chipped in Jordan. "But I wouldn't worry too much about him. One thing's for sure, knowing Billy, he would have found a way of getting out safely. You wait until we get back to school; you'll see."

After stretching their weary bodies and taking in a deep frosty breath, they moved quickly across the snow-covered lawn toward the path, blinking at the early morning sun piercing the snow-covered branches and dappling the hard-sodden snowy ground with pools of warmth and light.

Reaching the safety of the rusty gate, they paused once more to look back at the shattered and dilapidated hall before wrapping their arms around each other in a cozy little rag-tag group, pleased at last to be going home, and wondering what had become of Adam and Amy. And, not forgetting Billy . . .

## Chapter Thirty-Five

It was now daylight, and once again the sky was full of snow clouds blowing around in the wind; the faint rays of the sun were touching the tent, giving the brothers some additional warmth inside.

It was the sound of the back door being opened that disturbed the three boys from a deep and restless sleep.

"Wakey wakey, boys! Breakfast's all ready on the table, so get yourself up, and don't let it get cold," called their mother, leaving the back door open so the aroma of bacon and eggs floated in the early morning air toward the tent.

"Hey, you two, are you awake?" asked Jordan quietly, trying to keep his voice down. "You're not going to believe this, but I had one of the most horrible and weirdest dreams ever last night. I dreamed I was stuck in the old hall with you two and . . ."

"What are you talking about, Jordan?" asked a bleary-eyed James, struggling to sit up on his knees, rearranging his disheveled clothes.

"That's spooky, Jordan. I must have had the same horrid dream as you," interrupted Thomas. "Billy Three h-ha-shoo, sorry, was in my dream, and two other kids, whose names I can't remember for the life of me. You know what it's like when you wake up, within seconds you can't remember a flipping thing? And next time, Jordan, don't invite me to any more of your dreams again, it was horrible . . . ugh! Where's that awful disgusting smell coming from? And look at the both of you! Your faces and clothes are all covered in dust and mud . . . just hold on a minute . . . James, what's *that* moving around at the front of your sweater?"

"Boys, did you hear me? Your breakfast's on the table, and it's starting to get cold. Don't make me have to remind you again."

~~~~~